Lokte

By K.J. Bryen

Copyright © 2014 by K.J. Bryen

All rights reserved. This book or any portion thereof may not be reproduced or used in any manner whatsoever without the express written permission of the publisher except for the use of brief quotations in a book review. This is a work of fiction. Any resemblance to actual persons, living or dead, is purely coincidental.

Printed in the United States of America

First Printing, 2014

Cover image Copyright used under license from iStock.com.

K.J. Bryen
www.plungingintothenovel.com

Acknowledgments Page

I wrote the first version of this novel while I was attending college. It was the first novel I actually seemed to be getting through, and the whole time, I couldn't stop thinking how incredible awesome it was. Me, writing a novel! It had always been a dream of mine, but every day I got up early and fueled myself with coffee before sitting at that computer, a little more hope sprung within me. In a few months, I completed it. My first novel. I read over it . . . and cringed.

I knew I had to rewrite it. So there I was again, sitting at my computer every morning hoping that a second time might be better. It has been a long road, but after several coffee-induced comas and binges on chocolate, there it was. It was complete. Along the crazy ride, there were lots of people that deserve shout-outs for enduring all of my insanity.

My college roommates Alex, Vicki, and Aubrey, for allowing me to essentially become a hermit while they had fun outside actually breathing fresh air. Seriously, thank you for not breaking down my door and for disregarding my zombie-like behavior in the morning.

Mari Farthing, for editing the first part of *Lokte* and not making me cry with her revisions. Thanks for going easy me while still being honest in your critique. It helped a lot.

The Cyber Scribes, for providing support and critiques of my writing. What would I do without some honest writers around to tell me when my work is terrible?

My grandparents, for providing endless support and being willing to actually read my work.

The people from the Writers Café, for answering all of my stupid questions on publishing with the utmost patience. Also for providing so much insight into the world of publishing that I thought my brain may explode.

Ellie Essary, for giving me advice on the cover design after I'd spent several grueling hours staring at the computer screen and could no longer tell what looked good and what didn't.

Blaine Warren, for listening to all of my boring book updates and actually pretending to find them interesting. Seriously, I don't know how much you were listening, but you always offered sound advice when I needed it. Kudos, bro.

My mom, Kimberly Warren, for being one of my most honest critics, despite being my mother. I could not asked for a better, more honest mom.

My spouse, Adam Warren-Bryant, for being the most supportive, loving husband throughout many long hours staring at the computer screen. My love, the fact that you bear through my endless frustrations, rants, and constant desire to spoil my plots for you to see what you think, never ceases to amaze me. You are my inspiration.

Last, but certainly not least, my father, Darren Warren. Every time I strayed away from God, you were there to provide an example of strength, patience, and understanding. You not only introduced me to a world of Christian fiction, you helped me on the path to God, and for that, there are no words. I can only pray that I will someday be as strong and loving as you are. Thank you for making me the woman I am today.

With that said, I think its time to get on with it, am I right? So sit back, relax, and try to enjoy the result of my twisted imagination. I hope you have as much fun reading it as I did writing it.

Sincerely,

K.J. Bryen

Chapter Index

Part I: The Fall

Prologue- 11

Chapter One- 13

Chapter Two- 18

Chapter Three- 24

Chapter Four- 31

Chapter Five- 37

Chapter Six- 44

Chapter Seven- 51

Chapter Eight- 60

Chapter Nine- 66

Chapter Ten- 71

Chapter Eleven- 86

Chapter Twelve- 94

Chapter Thirteen- 99

Chapter Fourteen- 106

Part II: The Rise

Chapter Fifteen- 117

Chapter Sixteen- 126

Chapter Seventeen- 134

Chapter Eighteen- 141

Chapter Nineteen- 146

Chapter Twenty- 156

Chapter Twenty-One- 165

Chapter Twenty-Two- 174

Chapter Twenty-Three- 182

Chapter Twenty-Four- 189

Chapter Twenty-Five- 200

Bonus Story: "Unlocked," a short prequel to *Lokte*- 204

To my father, Darren, for teaching me that in every darkness, there is always light.

Part I: The Fall

Prologue

Thomas Jackson hung the phone silently on the receiver, his heart pounding like a drum in his chest. He was shaking. The news he received filled his body with dread, the shock spreading along his insides in a slow, creeping trickle. He wanted to move, but his feet seemed stuck to the hardwood.

His phone began to ring again, sending a loud noise throughout the house. He feared answering it . . . but it could be him.

He pressed the green, flashing button.

". . . Hello?"

"Thomas," a voice said. It was Sophia from church. She was old, and her words came out in sputters. "Have you checked on him?"

". . . What?" His mind was too fuzzy to process her question.

"I know this news is awful, but you need to check on your friend. Now."

His feet began to tingle. "You're right . . . I'm sorry. I-I'm heading there now."

Tom hung up the phone and forced himself forward, his shoes clunking loudly as he exited the house. Darkness shrouded the city street. His weak legs formed long, earnest strides across the concrete as buildings zoomed past in a blurry whirl, the night air blowing drops of water on his flushed face. Streetlamps illuminated the sidewalk, flashing him with sudden jolts of yellow light beneath the clouded sky.

Why had he hesitated before? He had to get there soon; his friend needed him. He pressed even harder against his sore limbs, the world seeming to dissolve around him.

It felt like ages before he finally turned on that familiar street. The tiny white house loomed ahead, its red door slightly ajar. He leapt on the concrete steps and past the front yard where the grass was beginning to turn a murky brown. He barreled inside.

The house was dark, with a few pieces of furniture flipped over, and broken glass scattering the tan carpet.

"Hello?! It's me, Tom. Are you there? HELLO?!"

Silence. A sudden crack of thunder boomed, and lightning flashed outside the dim windows. Steady drops of rain pelted the roof.

His chest still heaving, he bent down and grabbed a broken frame lying on the floor. He stared at the picture with a heavy heart.

"Lord," he whispered, another strike of thunder sounding out behind him. "Only you can help him now. Please help him."

Outside, beyond his scope of hearing, a woman began to laugh, her high-pitched cackle resounding into the night sky.

Chapter 1

Marianne Garcia walked down a cold hallway, riddled with oddly shaped doors. Small blue ones, large red ones, circular pink ones. She hugged her side for warmth. She tried to open the doors, but they were all locked. If she could just get into one of them, perhaps she could escape this painful cold . . .

Finally, she came upon one that was ajar. She stopped in front of it. It was large and boxy, painted a dark espresso brown that looked black in the dull light. Fear trickled through her. She didn't know what lay beyond this door. What if it was worse than the cold? What if she got locked in a freezer, or torn to shreds? But she had to know. Reluctantly, she pushed on it. It swung open slowly, sounding out the eerie creaking of rusty hinges. She peered inside, and . . .

Nothing. There was nothing but blackness. This irritated her. She stepped forward, her feet traveling over the threshold . . . and into nothing. She gasped as she realized there was no floor. She tried to steady herself, but it was too late. Her body unwillingly leaned forward and she began to fall. For what seemed like several minutes, the air whipping around her, her scream echoing off invisible walls. She was plummeting, but to where? Did a hard, rocky ground wait to splatter her to pieces? Or would she continue to fall, forever doomed to plunge through this dark hole?

Finally, she spotted it. Orange lights flickering beneath her. This was it. She was going to die in this abyss. She wondered if anyone would miss her.

She felt it before she saw it. She hit it feet first, her body submerging in a pool of clear, fresh water. She pressed her limbs against the resisting waves and kicked herself to the surface. As her head broke to the cool air, she wiped the drops from her eyes and peered at her surroundings.

She was in a cave. A round, rocky cave with torches illuminating the walls. Something red was dripping from the rocks. It trickled all around the cavern, appearing like dark red fire. She looked down.

The water, which had been glistening and clear before, had turned to blood. Hot, sticky blood. She was covered in it; her whole body, like the walls, dripped with it.

She then began to giggle. Uncontrollable, maniacal laughter erupted from her, though she could not place what was funny. The mad laughter got louder and louder, rising up through the blood-stained cave.

Marianne woke up in a cold sweat. Her alarm clock flashed red numbers: 4:58 a.m., three hours before she was supposed to wake up. She was too shaken to go back to sleep. She placed a trembling hand on her bedside lamp and turned on the shaded light. She wiped the sweat from her forehead and walked to her kitchen, where she poured herself a glass of water. She then went to her window, sitting down on her rickety, velvet chair and peering down at the street below her. It was not a great view of New York City. Dingy buildings stood opposite to her apartment, blocking any chance of a skyline. Still, she liked sitting there. It comforted her when she began to feel lonely.

Across from her apartment building, a man blended into the shadow of a streetlamp, gazing into Marianne's window. Even from three stories below, he could see her clearly. Wavy, black hair in disarray, circles beneath her dark eyes, tiny beads of sweat on her caramel-colored skin. The nightmares must have started.

This filled him with satisfaction. Of course, it happened to many of his victims; they had bad dreams right before he made his presence known. It was amazing what the human subconscious could predict. He liked that they sensed him.

He waited, perched in the shadows of the night. Yes, the time was close. He would soon meet Marianne face-to-face. Then he would take her.

Up in her apartment, Marianne began to feel like she was being watched. She looked down at the street, but could not spot anything peculiar. It was probably just paranoia.

Still, just to be safe, she closed the curtain.

~~~

"Ms. Marianne, I'm hungry."
"Ms. Marianne, he stole my toy!"
"Ms. Marianne, when can we go home?"
"Ms. Marianne, Michael peed on the floor."

At the daycare, requests from the children seemed unending. There were less staff members than usual, and the children seemed to increase their demands accordingly.

Her phone began to ring, playing a contemporary pop song. The children at the daycare began to sing obnoxiously. She shushed them and hurried out of the room, answering on the third ring.

"Hello?" She sounded more exasperated than she meant to.

"Hey!" her talent agent Christopher Ballard greeted. "How's my favorite actress?"

Marianne had received a BFA in Acting from the University of Kansas before moving to New York. She immediately scouted out an agent and signed a contract with Christopher Ballard, who believed she had something special about her. He seemed to be the only one though, because she had been working at the daycare for two years, with no acting roles to show for it.

She forced a smile. "Oh not too bad, Chris."

"Excellent, excellent. Hey, you know that play you auditioned for last week?"

How could she not? A week prior, she had auditioned for the main role in a little Off-Broadway play. It was a small theatre, so she was hoping that would increase her chances.

He went on before she could reply: "Well unfortunately they went with another girl. But hey, don't let that get you down! Some of the most famous Broadway stars had years of rejections before landing their big role. Just hang in there, Mari. Your name will be in the blinking lights of Broadway, count on it!"

She barely registered any of his pep talk. All she could hear was the sound of her heart beating in her chest, her stomach churning with the pain of rejection. She muttered a thank you and hung up.

She was digging in a cluttered cupboard, mulling over the conversation, when a voice rung out behind her:

"Crazy day, huh?"

She turned around and smiled. It was her coworker Emily, blonde hair pulled back in a loose bun, dark rimmed glasses hanging off the brim of her nose. Her hands were placed casually on the edge of her apron, as if the chaos was not phasing her at all. Marianne liked Emily. She was the closest thing to a friend she had in New York.

"Yeah," Marianne replied. "And I'm running on four hours of sleep."

"Me too, but probably not for the same reason."

She rolled her eyes. "You work *here*. How can you afford to go out so much?"

Emily grinned. "I can't. Totally worth it, though."

A child tugged on Marianne's apron. She dug in the cupboard again and pulled out a Styrofoam cup. She filled it with water and handed to the child.

"In fact, I'm gonna go out tonight. Wanna join?"

Marianne paused.

"Oh come on, Mari!" Emily urged, as if sensing the potential no. "It's a Friday night. Put down your screenplays and live a little."

She had a point. Marianne had developed the habit of staying home, cuddled her blanket and reading plays, screenplays, or scripts. She wasn't trying to be anti-social. As a striving actress, she wanted to familiarize herself with theatre and film as much as possible.

But it certainly didn't help her social life.

"Well . . ." Marianne replied slowly. ". . . alright, I'm in."

They didn't notice the shadow that passed by the window.

Chapter 2

They started off with drinks, then headed out for a night of dancing. At the club, Mari sipped on a virgin strawberry daiquiri. She had already had two beers at the bar, and that was plenty for her. Marianne wasn't a big drinker. "Don't you go too far with that alcohol now," her mother had always warned her. "You drink too much, you're gonna wake up in a stranger's bed."

Her mother, who took on being a single mother with pride. Her mother, bravely battling cancer from several states away. If only Mari could be with her. But to go back to the Kansas countryside would be admitting she couldn't make it as an actress. And she couldn't bring herself to do that.

Emily downed a gin and tonic while sitting with her back to the table, her feet propped up on a stolen chair. Her lacy top was sagging on her shoulders, and her leather skinny jeans hugged her tiny thighs. She was already tipsy from vodka shots at the bar. Her body swayed gently back-and-forth. Meanwhile, the lights in the club flashed different colors; green, red, blue, purple, green again. The hip hop blared to a deafening volume, and the open dance floor was riddled with a tangle of barely clothed bodies, hugging each other to the beat of the music.

"You know, Mari," Emily slurred, glasses sliding off her nose. "You really should have worn something different. I mean, whose going to sleep with you, wearing that?"

Marianne looked down at her outfit. It was true, her dress did not scream provocative. It was a modest, plain blush-colored dress that contrasted against her honey skin. Long sleeves, a scoop neck, and a lace back. Pretty, but maybe not club material.

"I thought you liked this dress," Marianne countered.

"Yeah, for like shopping and stuff, not for *here*." She lingered a little too long on the last word. "I mean, don't you want to score with some hot guy tonight?"

"No! I'm saving myself, you know that."

"Oh yeah. I'm the one who wants that."

Marianne smiled.

"But I mean, come on," she continued. "You've already done it before, so what's the point?"

"That was only one guy, and now I want to save myself for marriage. I don't know, I always regretted it with him, and I want the next time to be special . . ."

Emily was no longer listening.

"Hey, let's go dance! If I'm lucky, I'll get noticed by a tall, handsome stranger."

Marianne laughed as Emily tugged fiercely at her arm, flinging her onto the floor just as a new, upbeat pop song began to play. The two girls then began dancing, letting the lights and the music rush over them like a tidal wave.

At the edge of the dance floor the man in black watched, his head tilted slightly as he paced around the perimeter. Her friend moved herself wildly to the music as if her body was a set of drums. But Marianne had a sensuality to her. Her hips swayed fluidly with the notes, her torso acting as a perfect metronome. The sight was intoxicating.

Her friend found a tall, blonde male companion as her dance partner after a few songs. Someone had asked Marianne to dance as well, but he was short, and his voice unnaturally high pitched. The man in black smirked as he watched the pair. While the boy could not keep his eyes off her gracefully moving body, she peered anxiously around the room, waiting for a chance to escape. As she should have; he was not worthy of her. But she would be taken by someone who was. Quite soon.

Marianne finally made it over to her friend, who was inching towards the edge of the dance floor, her dance partner's hand in hers.

"Well, Don here has offered to show me his Manhattan apartment," Emily gushed with excitement. "You don't mind, do you Mari?"

He could see the tension in Marianne's neck. Still, she replied, "Of course not. I'll see you Monday."

Emily practically leapt towards the exit, her hand clasped tightly around Don's. Marianne stood awkwardly at the edge of the dance floor for a moment before her short companion waddled up behind her.

"So do you want another dance, or do you want to take this somewhere private?" the guy asked with raised eyebrows.

The man in black wanted to laugh.

"Um, I'm actually really tired."

The disappointment was clear on the guy's face.

"But I had a nice time. It was really, really nice meeting you."

He seemed unsure of what to do. "Alright. Well, can I see you home?"

"No, that's okay. Thank you."

With that, they gave each other a wave, and she began walking towards the club's double doors.

Marianne, at night, alone. This could be his chance. The man in black trailed behind her at a safe distance, weaving between bodies before breaking out into the cool night air.

She did not search for a cab. Instead she walked along the tainted sidewalk, arms crossed in front of her, purse hanging loosely off her shoulder. He was astounded at how simple she was making this. Walking in a questionable neighborhood at night, by herself? It was too easy.

Meanwhile, Marianne began to feel unhinged. This man, dressed in all black had been following her since the club. She knew she should have called a cab. She started to pick up the pace, her heels clicking against the concrete. She could see a busier street ahead. If she could just make it there . . .

Suddenly, a burly man stepped out of the alleyway in front of her. Loose, dingy clothes, a brown handlebar mustache, face pressed into a scowl. He had a sleek pistol in his hand, pointed directly at her chest.

"Give me your purse," he commanded quietly.

The man in black stopped for a moment and smiled. The girl was shaking with fear as she muttered, "Please, don't . . ."

"Just give it to me!" the guy yelled.

This was his opportunity. He moved swiftly from behind her, stepping in front of Marianne protectively.

"Leave her alone."

The mugger seemed surprised at first, then narrowed his gaze. "Yeah? Well maybe I should kill you *and* your girlfriend . . ."

His reaction was quick. He swept his arm in the air and struck the mugger's hand, causing the gun to skid onto the sidewalk. He then grabbed him by the neck and pulled him close, so their faces were only inches apart.

"Look into my eyes," he whispered lowly.

He did. The burly man looked into those dark brown eyes, and suddenly, another vision began to form. The man in black was showing him his face; his true face, the one just beneath his fragile human exterior. His eyes went wide with fear, but he couldn't pry himself away. He could not stop gazing upon the horrific sight, like one peering into the face of their murderer.

The man in black let him go quickly. The gunman collapsed on the concrete; his eyes were still bugged, his body shaking uncontrollably. With a whimper, he stumbled up and ran down the street until he could turn, disappearing from view.

He turned to face Marianne. Her body was stiff and her mouth hung open slightly. He liked seeing her afraid.

"You . . . you saved me," she muttered.

He didn't particularly care about her safety, but he would have to act.

"Are you alright, miss?"

She nodded slowly. "Yes. Thank you."

"It is no trouble at all."

"No, it is. You stepped in front a bullet for me. I mean, that was . . . is, is there any way I can repay you?"

He had to keep from smiling.

"Well, a cup of coffee would be nice. Do you mind if I see you home?"

"Actually, I would love that. Thank you."

They began walking down the sidewalk together.

"I'm Marianne, by the way. Marianne Garcia."

She held out a perfectly polished hand. He took it in his and shook it, offering her a cordial smile. "Nice to meet you, Marianne. I'm Logan Lokte."

Chapter 3

Marianne's mind raced. It was a good night, up until that horrible man tried to mug her, pointing a gun at her and threatening her life.

But Logan Lokte, a complete stranger, stepped in front of the gun and saved her. Why had she been so paranoid about him following her? He was an absolute hero . . . and handsome, too. He had a rugged look about him; dark hair, defined eyebrows, muscular build, narrow, penetrating eyes. He wore a fitted, button-up black shirt that framed his body, and his straight bangs hung over his eyes, fashioned like that of a rock star. He appeared to be in his late twenties, only a few years older than Marianne.

She wished he weren't so terribly attractive. It made it difficult for her to talk.

"So, do you save people often?" she asked as they turned a corner.

"All the time," he replied with a smirk. She couldn't tell if he was being serious or not.

"Where are you from?"

"Here, and you?"

"Kansas."

"Oh? Where in Kansas?"

"Well, originally I'm from southern Kansas, but I spent four years at the University of Kansas in Lawrence."

"What did you study?"

"... Acting," she responded hesitantly. People often rebuked her dream of being an actress on Broadway.

He peered ahead thoughtfully. "Doubt thou the stars are fire; doubt that the sun doth move; doubt truth to be a liar . . ."

"But never doubt I love." She smiled. "*Hamlet.*"

"Yes. A beautiful story."

"Tragic, though."

He tilted his head curiously. "Are you referring to the ending?"

"No. I'm talking about Ophelia. Hamlet wanted revenge more than he wanted her, and it cost her both her sanity and her life. She lost everything."

He nodded, as if turning the words around in his head. "Well Marianne, acting is a great pursuit. I'm sure you'd make a marvelous actress."

She grinned. She liked the way he talked; how he listened, treated her like she mattered. She didn't get that often in New York.

They arrived at her apartment moments later. Her five hundred square foot studio was up three flights of stairs. Though she was used to the walk, she always had to catch her breath. She unlocked the door and pushed it open, revealing a quaint living space. Clothes were strewn over the floor, and the "bedroom" was blocked off by a curtain, but it was nicely put together. A small, sleek white couch, modest flat screen television, a wooden chair by the window, quartz kitchen countertops. Small, but modern.

A very handsome man, in her apartment, in the middle of the night; she was suddenly in a frenzy. She rushed up to him as he sat on the couch.

"Can I get you anything to drink? Oh, coffee! Right. I'll get that for you."

He appeared amused. "Thank you."

She shuffled over to the kitchen and began pouring the water for the pot, which she spilled all over the counter. She wanted to hit herself for acting so silly. She supposed she was still excited from the near death experience from earlier. Not to mention, she *never* had men over, especially those who looked and acted like superheroes.

She brought him a cup of black coffee, sitting down across from him with a cup of hot tea in her hand. They were quiet for a moment.

"So what do you do?" Logan asked politely. "Besides acting."

"Well, right now I'm working at a daycare. I did a lot of babysitting through college, so it seemed like a good starting job. What about you?"

". . . I do a lot of things," he said slowly. "Primarily, I suppose you could call me . . . a salesman, of sorts."

"Oh? What do you sell?"

He leaned forward suddenly, his dark eyes earnest. "Marianne, you must be wondering why I wanted to have coffee with you."

Her heart quickened. "Why did you?"

"Because I saw something in you," he responded without missing a beat. "Even without meeting you, I could tell you were a woman who sells herself short, who settles for less than she's worth. I think you deserve better."

His words stung her heart. He acted as if he knew her. But he couldn't . . .

Could he?

He set his coffee on the table and clasped his hands together. "The things I sell . . . they make people better. They give them the ability to obtain their heart's deepest desires. I request that you keep an open mind, Marianne. It is unorthodox, but also incredible. I simply ask that you allow me to maintain your company for the next three weeks. If I have not convinced you by then, I will be out of your life forever. But believe me when I say I genuinely want to help you. You deserve everything in this world. Will you hear my proposal?"

Her breath caught in her throat. Marianne had never heard a speech so short, so elegant . . . so confusing. What did he mean, proposal? He didn't even know her. What made her think she was special enough to deserve anything? Lost for words, she said the only thing she could think of.

"Okay."

~~~

Logan left with a sense of smug satisfaction. She was on his hook, now all he had to do was reel her in. It would take time, of course, and possibly a level of seduction. They were often reluctant when they heard the price. But it didn't matter. They always gave in. Always.

At that moment, a ripple of confusion fluttered through his body. This was completely normal. Ever since his change, he had spastic thoughts; wonderings of whether it was him, Logan Lokte thinking a certain thought, or the thing that lived inside him. It was a valid question. It seemed like the longer he went on, the more joined the two beings in his flesh became.

Still, his old self would occasionally burst out, either in a thought or action; a sudden gasp of air, as if taking in a final breath. Perhaps it was. Perhaps every inch of who he once was would soon die, slowly fading away until he was nothing but a bad memory resting in the deep, buried reservoirs of his skull.

Good riddance.

~~~

Marianne smiled as she poured herself a cup of steaming coffee. She added sugar and cream, creating a sweet, comforting concoction before sitting down by her window. It was nine o' clock, and the sun had risen above the concrete buildings. She pushed a strand of hair from her face, her mind stirring with memories of the night previous.

Logan Lokte. She could not get him out of her mind. His dark, perfectly imperfect hair, his strong arms, and the way he leapt in front of that gun. He was like a knight in shining armor, come to rescue her from her five hundred square foot dungeon.

Of course, this was absurd. He barely seemed interested in her. And that sales pitch? What was that all about? He never said what he was selling. What was so important that he would want to stick around for three weeks? What could he possibly have that would make her life so much better?

She wanted to talk about him to someone. But who? The only person in New York she knew was Emily, and Emily had a lot of friends. For her, Marianne was just another girl to go to the club with. She could call her old college friends, but they had all moved elsewhere. She'd barely spoken to them since graduation.

It seemed there was only one person she could call.

She punched the number into her cellphone. It rang twice before a weak voice traveled through the speaker.

"Hello?"

Marianne took a sip of coffee before answering. "Hi, Mom."

"Well, hi girl. How are you?"

It was obvious that the chemotherapy was doing a number on her. Still, her mom always loved a call from her only daughter. Marianne did her best to sound encouraging.

"I'm great," she lied. "I've been getting a lot of auditions lately, so things are good. What about you? Are you okay?"

"Oh, I'm holding on. You know sickness can't get the best of me."

Despite her upbeat tone, Marianne was frowning. "I know."

"In fact, once this passes, I'm going to go back to work. I hear those kids are missing me."

Her mother was an elementary teacher at a rural school in Kansas. Ms. Garcia, the kids called her. She possessed a stern kindness that demanded both respect and love from her children. Marianne would know. She grew up with it.

"That would be great."

"Yeah it would. I'm tired of lying in bed all the time. But enough about me. Anything new with my favorite daughter?"

She smiled. "Well yes, actually. The craziest thing happened to me the other night. You see, there was this guy . . ."

"A guy?" her mother's small voice went up in pitch. "It's about time my Mari got back in the game! Tell me about him."

So she told her. She told her everything, except she replaced the mugger with an obscene guy at the club, and she didn't mention the gun. She didn't want her to get worried. Once she was finished, her mom was in awe.

"So, a handsome stranger defended your honor, had coffee with you in your apartment, and told you he had a *proposal*?"

"That's right."

". . . Are you sure he didn't mean a real proposal?"

Marianne laughed. "We'll see when we go to lunch tomorrow."

"Well that's great! I'm really happy for you, honey." Her voice gave out on the last word. Marianne knew it was time to let her rest.

"I'm going to let you go, Mom. Feel better! I love you!"
"I love you too, Mari. Goodbye."
"Bye."

She set the phone beside her and sipped on lukewarm coffee, her mind wandering with the wispy summer clouds. On one hand, Logan made her feel like a love-struck school girl. On the other, there was something about him, something distinct that gave her a bad taste on the tip of her tongue. She couldn't pin point what it was, but it could only be categorized as a bad feeling.

She suddenly remembered last night's nightmares.

Chapter 4

Marianne and Logan met at the restaurant Amy's Café. It was a skinny hub squeezed between two larger buildings. The inside was modeled after the 1950's, with bold pops of color and pictures of Elvis and Marilyn Monroe. There were only a few booths and a couple of stools to sit at, but it had the best burgers Marianne had ever tasted. It was what her mother called, "a gem in a thorn bush." Marianne had taken her mother there the one time she visited New York, over a year ago. She wished they could see each other more, but neither had the money to travel.

      They sat at a little red booth, tucked in a corner against the wall. Marianne wore a pretty, white sundress with a tan belt and wedges, her hair pulled back and cascading into waves down her shoulders. Logan had on a loose, black shirt that formed a V on his chest; the short sleeves showed off his defined biceps, which seemed to flex every time he moved. He finished off the look with a pair of dark wash jeans, black shoes, and a plain black bracelet that clipped on his wrist. Even in his casual apparel, he looked like a rock star.

They began with small talk. They talked about the weather and how great Amy's Café was. By the time their food came out, Marianne was more curious about him than ever.

"So what is this proposition you were telling me about?" she asked. "You wouldn't tell me the other day."

"It is something that needs to be heard . . . in doses." His eyes met hers, and he smiled. "But before I tell you anything, you have to tell *me* something. What is it in this world that you want most?"

She stared at him blankly. "I'm sorry?"

"I know that is a personal question, but it must be answered before I can explain my proposal. What do you want most in this world?" When she was reluctant to reply, he placed a gentle hand on hers. "You can trust me."

She hesitated. She had never been asked that question before. It was like telling a deep, dark secret to a complete stranger.

But Logan wasn't a stranger, was he?

". . . I want my mother to be cured of cancer. And I want to be a famous actress on Broadway."

He nodded. "Well, Marianne, I can give you exactly that."

She gazed at him incredulously. "How?"

"Oh, all will be revealed in good time. But today, I want you to think about that. Think about what it would be like to have all your dreams come true . . . and realize that it's possible."

She couldn't withhold the next question that came out of her mouth. ". . . What *are* you?"

To that, he simply smiled.

Marianne was dumbfounded. When he had first told her of a proposal, she assumed that it was something tangible, something real. But his explanation was incredible. Curing someone of cancer? Securing her fame, when she hadn't acted in two years? She couldn't tell if he was crazy or not. But one thing was sure, beyond a doubt . . .

Logan Lokte was not a normal man.

~~~

Marianne's head reeled as she took the bus to work the next day.

Logan's promises gave her hope, but they also filled her with doubt. She wanted it all to be true, but she was a realist. People didn't get cured of terminal diseases, and girls from Kansas didn't become Broadway stars. To achieve all of this Logan would have to have magic, and she *knew* that wasn't possible.

Right?

The bus rolled beneath her, bouncing her up and forcing her to grip tightly onto the metal pole. She was feeling particularly lonely that day. Sometimes it felt like she had no one in New York. Logan was just so mysterious and aloof, and she wondered if she would ever get on a more intimate level with him. Of course, she had Emily; she was the closest thing Marianne had to a friend. She wished the bus would go faster so that she could tell her about Logan.

Only weeks prior, she would have gone to God for comfort. Marianne had been a devout Christian since she was twelve years old. She found delight in a variety of denominations, and would have two or three churches that she attended regularly, usually Catholic, Methodist, or Evangelical. She enjoyed the various ways of worship, the different interpretations of scripture. She had even found two churches in the city: St. Mary's Catholic Church and St. Paul's Methodist Church. Although she enjoyed the services, the people there never opened up to her. They never invited her to Bible studies, never asked her to join potluck dinners. She felt like a ghost floating aimlessly in the back of the building.

As she stared at the long, dirt-ridden bus floorboard, she relished her old life. Her old friends from college, the weekly bible studies, the grueling rehearsals in the university theatre. There was a time when she had faith. When the weight of the world had not begun tumbling down on her fragile and weary spirit . . .

She just wanted to get to work.

Minutes later, the bus rolled to a stop. It was misting outside, creating a dense, wet fog. She threw a handful of change in the driver's jar and hopped onto the sidewalk. Only a block, and she could tell Emily about Logan.

She hurried into the one-story daycare, throwing her thin jacket off her shoulders. The children wouldn't arrive for thirty minutes, but the employees would already be there. She scanned the room. There was Cora, Aubrey, Lexi . . .

Where was Emily?

She rushed up to Lexi, who raised her eyebrows indifferently. The two had hardly spoken before.

"Hey, is Emily here yet?" Marianne asked.

"No, I haven't seen her."

She muttered a thanks as Lexi wandered to the other end of the room. *She's probably just running late,* Marianne told herself. *She'll be here in a few minutes.*

But a few minutes passed, and Emily never appeared through the glass door. She shifted uncomfortably. Several more minutes passed, and still no Emily. A full thirty minutes went by, and the children began pouring in. Marianne frowned.

Where is she?

~~~

Logan strolled through the streets of New York City, his hands shoved in his pockets and his eyes set ahead of him. A warm fog surrounded him, enveloping his body like a dense blanket. He loved days like this. During his old life, he liked them because they were relaxing, an equivalent to rainy days. Now it was different. Now they made him feel cloaked, like an unseen predator, ready to pounce on any unfortunate victim clouded within the mist.

He gazed at the bodies that trailed past him. All these people, going about their daily lives, as if he were just another aimless human. They didn't know. They couldn't see the darkness within him. If they knew, oh how they would tremble with fear . . .

He stopped for a moment and gazed into the transparent doors of the daycare. There was Marianne, busying herself with a hoard of whining children. How demeaning. A girl as beautiful and talented as her did not deserve to be a slave to the whims of children. Now, her friend; Emma? Evie? He couldn't remember her name. That obnoxious girl could serve little brats all her life, and be perfectly fit to do so.

Where was she, anyways?

At that moment, a rough finger tapped his shoulder. He whipped around.

A man stood behind him. Tall, blonde, with a strong jaw and defined muscles. He had on fitted brand-name clothes, and his hair was slicked back with fine gel. He looked familiar, but Logan could not place his face.

He stretched his arms out welcomingly, a huge grin spreading across cheeks. "Logan Lokte! It has been too long, my friend."

"Do I know you?" Logan asked coldly.

He frowned. "Oh come on, you don't remember me? Well, I was in a different body then, I suppose . . ."

Logan waited impatiently for further explanation.

"It's me! Sallos!"

His memory was instantly jogged. Sallos, of course! He had been present during Logan's change. Sallos had been in the body of a Middle Eastern man then with long, curly hair. But Logan *had* seen this body before. And quite recently, too . . .

"Sallos!" he replied with a smile. "How are you?"

"Things are great, Logan. I just took this form a year ago, and I couldn't be more happy with it. Actually, I saw you Friday night. I meant to say something, but I was a little preoccupied," he said with a wicked grin.

Now he remembered. He had seen Sallos at the club, dancing with Marianne's friend.

For goodness sake, what was her name?

Logan put a friendly hand on his shoulder and walked him down the misty sidewalk. "It is great to see you, my old friend. Tell me, how are your current conquests going?

Chapter 5

Marianne waited at the entrance to Central Park. The assortment of imported trees surrounded her as beautiful towers, their leaves forming into bright explosions of green that shone in the sunlight. She stood awkwardly by a metal park bench while tourists walked past her, gawking at the artificial beauty and capturing it with their over-sized cameras. She was dressed in a white, lace top tucked into a blue skirt that extended nearly to her knees, her hair pinned back and forming pretty curls down her shoulders.

      She was nervous. There was something about Logan that made her feel both giddy and frightened at the same time. She hoped he would show up. What was she thinking? Of course he would! He was the one who suggested Central Park. Plus, he had this offer he was trying to make her. This mysterious offer that she still knew nothing about . . . seriously, could he not just tell her upfront?

      She twirled a strand of hair around her finger. She was about to sit down on the metal bench, when she saw him. Logan Lokte, strolling into the park with such an air of cool confidence that it made her want to faint. A dark blue button up shirt rolled at the sleeves, nearly black jeans, all black shoes. He really had this punk-rock look down.

    A smile spread across his face. "You look lovely, Marianne."

Blush rushed to her cheeks. "Well, thank you."

He held out an arm.

"Shall we?"

Her heart fluttered within her. Grasping lightly onto his arm, they began walking, traveling along the side walk beside fresh beds of grass. Marianne had not ruled out the thought that Logan was crazy. He obviously believed he could make her famous and cure her mom of cancer. But somehow, it still felt right, her arm in his.

    Beside her, Logan felt a stirring, like a butterfly in his stomach. He grimaced at the feeling.

"And how has your day been?" he asked politely.

"Oh, as good as I suppose daycare can be," she replied. "Lots of screaming and dirty diapers."

"Always fun."

She giggled, but her smile quickly turned to a frown. "Though I haven't seen Emily since Friday."

"Emily?"

"One of my coworkers. She hasn't been to work all week, and I can't get a hold of her."

"I'm sure she will turn up." He sounded indifferent. She supposed he had every right to not care. It's not like he knew her.

"Yeah, probably."

They were silent for a moment. He began leading her, bringing her slightly to the right. She followed. They passed upon the hot sidewalk until they reached a large expanse of green grass. It was dotted with purple and white flowers that created tiny colorful blooms, like spots of color on a canvas. He took her there and reached into the satchel across his shoulder, pulling out a large, hand-sewn quilt. He spread it out on the grass.

He plopped down on it and motioned for her to sit.

She raised her eyebrows. "You're serious?"

"Oh, I would never joke about this."

She shook her head and sat down on the blanket, where Logan was peering ahead at the bright blue sky. She followed his gaze, her fingers digging into the soft, velvety material.

"This is a really nice quilt," she commented.

"Thank you. My mother made it."

"Oh really? Does she still sew?"

He seemed to think about this for a moment. "I don't know."

Marianne blinked. "What do you mean, you don't know?"

"Well truth be told, I haven't seen my mother in quite some time."

"Oh . . . I'm sorry."

"Don't be. She would not want to see me right now, anyways."

Marianne thought about trying to console him, but the knowing smirk on his face told her she didn't need to.

"Well, I guess I haven't seen my mother in a long time, either."

"How long has it been?"

"Almost two years now. But that's okay. We still talk every day, and she supports my dream."

"She should. Your dream is wonderful."

She smiled. "Thanks. It's kind of overdone, though."

"That's because adults like to fill children's minds with the belief that they can do anything they want, even if they're not good at it. Even if they don't have what it takes. So theatres fill up with the promising actors, and most of them fail. But you, Marianne, you do have what it takes."

She shook her head. "How could you possibly know that? You haven't even seen me act."

"I don't have to. All I have to do is look at you, and I can tell. Call it a gift."

"That's some gift. I can't tell anything about you."

He looked down at the quilt. "That's probably best for both of us."

"Why? I'd like to get to know you. Let's see. Maybe I can tell something . . ." Her eyes traced his body. "Well, I can tell you like dark clothes, and that you are different from any normal person. I know you're really charming. I can also think you have a past that you are running away from." She smiled. "Kind of like how I ran away from Kansas."

He was taken aback by the observation. Those kind eyes peered at him, and he couldn't help but smile back. "Not too far off, Mari."

The two turned their gazes toward the clouds, where the sun was just beginning to set over the horizon. The sky was riddled with slight traces of pink, swirled with blue like a piece of art.

"It's amazing, isn't it?" Logan wondered aloud.

"What is?"

"The beauty that humans can create when they manipulate nature. Look at these trees, these flowers; all of them have been imported from thousands of miles away. People found a way to ship them here, keep them alive, and created the most spacious, beautiful park in the country."

She looked ahead thoughtfully. "I thought you were talking about the sky at first."

"The sky holds no magnificence."

"What do you mean? You don't think nature, in its natural form, is beautiful?"

"Not at all. Perhaps it was immediately after its creation, but after several millenniums it still stands still, hardly changing, the same sky that every human views. There is no wonder in it, just familiarity.

It's what *people* build that is marvelous. People are always moving, always changing. They manipulate the world to their liking and take charge of their own destinies. The people who built this park, they didn't care that these trees belong in South Africa, or that those flowers originate in South America. They changed the natural order of things. They saw their collection, and it was good."

Marianne had never heard such opinions from anyone before. She had always admired nature as one of God's wonderful creations . . . she did see his point, but it made her uneasy.

"You have very interesting views" she muttered.

"You will see it my way."

"Why? Because of your offer?"

He turned to face her. "Have you done as I asked?"

"What? You mean imagine a perfect life? Sure. But it doesn't change anything. My life is far from it."

"It doesn't have to be."

"You honestly believe you can put me on Broadway and cure my mom of cancer?"

He cocked his head to the side. "You think I'm crazy, don't you?"

She hesitated.

"I'm not, you know."

She peered over at him and saw that his eyes were glowing like fire. "Do you want me to prove it?"

She wasn't sure what to say. "How . . ?"

"I'll show you."

He made a sudden move towards her. She flinched instinctively. He pulled back, then moved forward again slowly. He got behind her, him on his knees, her still sitting down. He put a gentle hand over her eyelids, the other resting comfortably on her hip. Her heart quickened. He was so close; she could feel his hot breath on her neck, sending chills down her spine. He put his lips to her ear.

"Close your eyes," he whispered.

She obeyed. The bright view of the park darkened. For a moment, all she could see was blackness. But then, a flicker. And another. Like pixels on a television, light began forming dots in the darkness, until they finally formed a full picture. A movie was playing inside her head; and it was incredible.

The scene featured her, surrounded by an array of old friends, family, and people she didn't know, adoring fans throwing books in her face and begging for her autograph. A red curtain was displayed in the background, lit by a dim red light that colored the surrounding area. Her agent watched from a distance, but no one was more proud than her mother. Her Mom stood, completely healthy, a strong hand clasped on her daughter's shoulder. She smiled, her black and gray streaked hair forming into beautiful curls around her face. In the middle of the crowd, her mother's eyes gleamed.

"You are more, Mari, than any mother could have asked for. I'm so proud of you."

Marianne wanted to cry. But before she could, the scene changed. There she was, standing on the stage of the Lyric Theatre in Broadway. She was absolutely radiant, dressed in a fitting, sparkly gown that slit down her calf. Her long hair was loose, but fashioned into perfect slinky waves, and her makeup was bold, her eyelids streaked like black wings. The theatre was jam packed, and past the blinding lights, she could only make out one face: her mother's. Cheeks full, hair long, sitting in a beautiful dress in the front row.

Confidence radiated from Marianne. She raised her arms up and, absorbing the stage lights like energy, she belted a song. Her voice boomed out of her tiny body and filled the theatre. Marianne had always been more of an actress than a singer, but in this vision, there were no qualms. She was a wonder. A star. Hundreds of eyes were on her, and she relished every minute of it as her voice echoed against the walls, seeming to carry past the theatre entrance and into the world beyond.

Marianne gasped. Sunlight flooded through her eyelids, and the world came at her in a slow haze. She was back in Central Park. Logan was beside her, his hand removed from her eyes.

"Marianne, are you okay?"

She realized that her face was wet. She hadn't noticed the tears streaming down her cheeks.

"I'm fine," she said while wiping a big wet glob from her eye. "That was amazing."

"I'm glad you enjoyed it."

"How did you do that?"

"Oh, you are not ready for that information yet. But it was spectacular, was it not?"

"Yes. I felt like I was on top of the world."

"And you can be. See, that is what I've been trying to tell you," he said, his voice rising in excitement. "You really can have all of these things. All you have to do is sign a contract."

"There's a contract?" Her head was still muddled with the beautiful images. "Is there something I'd be giving up in this contract?"

He frowned and leaned back. "Perhaps I will tell you . . . but not until our next meeting. For now, just remember what you've seen, and think about how it made you feel."

She sighed. Her body was lax from the experience, and she found herself plopping her head on Logan's chest. He was surprised at first. But then, a small smile stroked his cheek.

Chapter 6

Logan reveled in his experience at Central Park. The visions he had shown Marianne- he could see everything, each scene that she had unknowingly created in her head. All he had to do was show her what she wanted.

Marianne, signing autographs and listening to that touching speech by her mother; her on that stage, dressed like a rock star and belting with a voice like an angel. He wondered if she sounded like that in real life. He supposed it didn't matter. What mattered was that *she* heard it, and she now believed it was possible. She had even cried! Oh yes, the meeting was a complete, total success.

Despite his accomplishment, a nagging feeling pulled at him. He didn't like certain habits he had developed these past two meetings. When she spoke, he found himself leaning in . . . with *actual*, not feigned interest. When she walked, his eyes would immediately trail to her defined curves. He loved how she smelled like fresh rain. He noticed the tiny dimples in her smile. And when she leaned her head on him at Central Park, he had smiled, and not because of his success. He smiled, simply because he liked the feeling of her in his arms.

Disgusting.

He didn't know what was wrong with him. They had only met three times, for goodness sake! He had never had this problem with his other pursuits, and he had seduced some attractive girls. This must be a fluke. Yes, this was just an off day. Tomorrow, he would shake those dirty feelings and rid his mind of all things related to Marianne Garcia.

~~~

Logan walked to Marianne's apartment that upcoming Saturday.

Unfortunately, his plan had not worked. The wretched woman continued to stick in his mind like a plague. But he could not act unprofessional. He had a job to do, one that required logic, cunning, manipulation. It would demand all of his rhetoric ability, and for that, he needed to focus. No more lending toxic feelings towards this girl from nowhere-Kansas. He would tell her the full details of the deal today, and then convince her to accept, all in one swoop. It was a tall order, but what choice did he have? He had to rid himself of this poison before it spread like a disease.

He approached the plain three-story building that housed Marianne's apartment. He marched through the glass door and bounded up the flights of steep, wooden stairs that rattled dangerously with each stomp. Once he was at her doorstep, he stopped for a moment and took a deep breath. He knocked on the door.

"Come in," a small voice answered.

He smiled. He already knew what he was going to say, how he would manipulate his words to appeal to her darkest desires. He opened the door.

Marianne was waiting- but she didn't appear happy to see him. She was dressed in a baggy, stained t-shirt and shorts. Her thick hair was in disarray around her face, and her cheeks were red and puffy, tears extending all the way down and forming tiny puddles on her shirt.

Logan stopped. Normally when he saw someone cry, he had to fight back a sneer. *What weakness*, he would think. But this time, another feeling crept within his stomach, a feeling that tasted like coarse rocks on his tongue.

Oh no. Is this . . . pity?

He had not felt such a trivial emotion since the day of his change four years prior. It felt strange to him, like an old memory creeping up from a distant past.

He didn't like it.

"I . . . what's wrong?"

She sniffled and turned away. "Nothing. I'm fine."

He stood awkwardly for a moment before shutting the door behind him and walking up to the couch. As he sat down beside her, he tried to find the right words. Normally he would have used this occasion to play on her vulnerability, but the horrible pity that dug in his gut told him to comfort her . . . and after all these years, he had quite forgotten how.

"Come on, Marianne. Tell me what's wrong."

She wiped a tear from her eye. "I'm sorry. It's just . . . it's about Emily."

A foreboding shiver traveled up his spine. "Yes?"

"Well, she's been gone for over a week now, with no sign of her . . . she's been declared missing."

Logan wanted to sigh with relief. "So, they haven't found her yet?"

"No. They say she hasn't been seen since last Friday. Gosh Logan, I was with her that night. What if I was the last person to see her? What if something awful happened to her? I knew I should have asked her to stay! She could be lost, or trapped, or worse . . . and it would be my fault."

He placed a hand on her thigh. "This is not your fault. She was determined to go no matter what you said. You wouldn't have been able to change anything."

She started to nod when a quizzical look formed on her face. "How do you know she was determined to go?"

He scolded himself silently.

"I can tell from your description of her," he lied coolly. "She seems like the type of person who just does what they want."

She seemed to accept that answer. "Yeah, I guess she is. But if I had . . ."

"Stop. There is nothing you could have done. No matter what happened, you cannot blame yourself. It's no one's fault. Okay?"

She nodded slowly. She then placed a gentle hand on his. He looked at those tear stained eyes, her full red lips. No, this couldn't happen again. He had to feel indifferent about her.

"Thank you, Logan. You're such a blessing to me."

His resolve seemed to crumble within him. A blessing. She had called *him* a blessing. If only she knew what his real intentions were, what he planned to do. She would think twice about throwing around that word.

Still, why did he find himself wanting to be a blessing?

The being inside him shuddered with contempt.

He did what he could to cheer her up. They made coffee, talked a little bit, and then agreed they should go out for ice cream. He could feel the force within pulling angrily at him. It kept reminding him of his job, urging him to bring up the deal. He ignored it. When it finally understood he was not giving in, it became spastic, throwing random, disturbing images in his mind. They became more frequent as the day went on, and it began to get very distracting. Finally, as Marianne and him sat at a tiny table in the dessert shop, he couldn't take it anymore.

He forced a smile. "Would you excuse me, while I go to the restroom?"

"Oh, sure."

He got up and walked towards the bathroom. He charged through the swinging door and supported his body on the sink, peering at himself in the mirror.

Would you stop it?! He practically screamed at the being. *I know what I'm doing.*

Have you forgotten a certain deal you made four years ago? It hissed in his ear. *You have a Master. We have a Master.*

I know. I'm not breaking that deal.

Of course you're not! You signed a contract. We both know there is only one way to erase your signature, and you are not going down that road again, are you?

You know I won't, he said with a frown.

Good! Then you must do your job. Breaking a contract is not the only thing that can entice our Master's wrath. You are walking on thin ice, Logan Lokte; hope that the girl doesn't get caught in the middle.

Anger rose up within him. *You leave Marianne out of this! I'm not threatening her. But the Master might.*

. . . Look. Neither of you need to worry. I am going to do my job. But to do that, I need to gain her trust, right? I think one day without discussing business will help her to believe I don't have alternative motives. Right?

. . . Perhaps, it said slowly.

Good. Then all is going according to plan. I will not let these feelings get in the way of anything; believe me, I can use them to my advantage. Marianne Garcia will be ours. But if you want that to happen, I need you to stop harassing me.

There was a long pause. *You had better go through with it, Logan. Otherwise, you will have to face both of us.*

He nodded at his own reflection. *Understood.*

With that, the voice died in his head.

Everything within him was swirling. This was not normal. Usually the being and he worked in tandem, thinking the same thoughts, doing the same things. They were a perfect team, one in mind and body. He had not had an actual conversation with it in over three years.

As he leaned wearily against the sink, a large man with a bushy mustache walked out of one of the stalls. The guy walked up to a neighboring sink, washing his hands while humming an unrecognizable tune. Suddenly, his eyes darted to Logan's reflection. He looked him up and down, his thick eyebrows pulled together.

"Hey," he said gruffly. "You alright?"

It was a valid question. Logan was panting hard, his face strained and drenched in cold sweat.

"I'm fine," he replied shortly.

The large man let out a humph, then dried his hands before walking out of the bathroom. Logan could not see Marianne looking this way. He rushed over to the paper towel dispenser and patted a sheet against his forehead, which came off soaked. He took a couple of deep, steady breaths and tried to smile in the mirror. Better. He let go of the edge of the porcelain sink and forced himself out of the restroom.

Marianne was waiting, her ice cream now gone and her head rested on her hand. As he sat down, she sighed with relief.

"There you are! Are you okay? You were in there for fifteen minutes."

"I was?" He had not kept track of time.

"Yeah. I thought you might have gotten lost," she joked.

"I'm sorry. I was feeling a little sick."

"Oh, I'm sorry. Do you need to leave?"

"No, no," he replied quickly. "I'm fine now."

She looked down at her empty bowl then looked up again, her eyes gleaming. "Logan, I want to thank you again for being here today. I know you didn't have to try and comfort me, but you did. You have no idea how much it means to me."

His heart filled with warmth. "It's my pleasure."

"I really do appreciate it. We barely know each other. You didn't owe me anything." She peered down again, a shy blush spreading across her cheeks. "I want to ask you something."

"Anything."

"Well . . . there's this banquet next week. It helps actors get connections and meet producers and such. I know it's not really your thing, but it's really fancy, and I was wondering . . . if you wanted to go with me."

He blinked. "You mean as a date?"

"Yes."

He could feel the being rising in anger again. *No,* it insisted. *No, no, no . . .*

He pretended to peer ahead thoughtfully, as if he were carefully weighing his options. He then looked back at her, gazing intensely into her chocolate brown eyes.

"I'd love too."

Chapter 7

Marianne sat on the velvet plush chair, her fingers reaching for the fabric nervously. She had more nightmares last night. They were similar to her other ones; her covered in blood, laughing maniacally. They weren't helping her current state of stress, and they certainly weren't easing her mind about this audition.

Another audition. She had taken off work to perform a monologue in front of that familiar row of chairs, full of stern-faced judges with tiny water bottles. All judge panels appeared the same to her: critical and terrifying.

She supposed there was something different about this panel, though. This time, she was actually auditioning for Broadway.

It was already fifteen minutes past her scheduled audition time. What was taking them so long?

Her mind was jittery as she stared at the blank white walls of the backstage room. At another time in her life, she would have spent this time drinking hot tea, looking over her lines, praying fervently.

Now she was doing everything but the latter. It was a shame, too. Praying had always given her immense comfort before. It helped her go into her audition with peace, with the belief that no matter what, everything would be okay.

She wasn't sure when her faith had begun to diminish. Perhaps it was when those fervent prayers all ended in rejections. Maybe it was when the people at her church discussed getting together for a retreat that weekend- and failed to invite her. When her mom never got healed, despite her prayers, or when this city that was supposed to provide hope only offered emptiness. Perhaps it happened when her coworkers at the daycare gave her the cold shoulder, or when her several attempts at connecting with others ended in disaster. When her nights began being spent at home or in Central Park, a screenplay in her hand as she gazed at the setting sun . . .

Maybe she should have gone to L.A.

She missed the old days. She missed that blind faith, her friends huddled around her, encouraging her, even in the worst of times. It was really hard to be faithful without anyone to help her. She could probably call her old friends, but what could they do? They were on opposite ends of the country, and she hadn't talked to them in two years. They probably didn't have room for her in their lives anymore.

Maybe this was a test. Or maybe God was punishing her for something. But she didn't know what she was being punished for, and if it were a test, she certainly had not passed. Maybe she was being punished for not passing the test?

Her head throbbed. She put a hand to her temple and took a gulp of green tea. She certainly wanted to trust God, but years of heartache had created dark cynicism within her soul. It ate the hope within her like a parasite. But if she could not place her faith in God . . . then in who?

"Marianne Garcia?" a voice rung out.

She jumped to her feet. The red-head with glasses looked her up and down with indifference, dark circles etched under her eyes.

"They're ready for you."

She felt her heart skip a beat. With shaking legs, she followed the woman through the black curtain that led to the little Broadway stage. Her heels clicked against the hard wooden floor, the stage lights nearly blinding her. She looked upon the panel of judges: all successes in the performing world. How had they done it? Did they start here, standing awkwardly in front of their own team of critiques? She gazed at the stern faces, so like the other ones she'd seen, and forced a smile.

"Hello, my name is Marianne Garcia, and I will be performing a monologue from the modern Broadway play, *Hope*."

No smiles. She took a quiet, bracing breath and set her arms at her sides. Then, staring just above the panel's heads at the white light ahead, she began speaking.

~~~

Logan Lokte had snuck into the theater, silent and unseen. He was shrouded in shadow, sure the stage lights would conceal his presence from Marianne. He watched. It was a dramatic monologue, full of longing and despair. It had ups and downs, the character conflicted and the tone constantly changing. She produced tears that fell like waterfalls, creating mascara-riddled lines down her cheeks. She moved her hands at the right times, and stayed still when appropriate. She looked beautiful. She wore a black halter dress that flowed out and cut off at the knees. A sparkling necklace traced her neck, and a bright shade of red lined her lips. It was the perfect mix of sensuality and professionalism that an audition calls for.

How had she not landed a role yet?

His state of awe was interrupted by a voice behind him:

"A fan of the theater, are you Logan?"

He turned around. Sallos stood behind him, a smug look lining his handsome face.

"I am when it involves my clients," Logan said dryly.

"Oh, so *this* is your current escapade. She's a pretty little thing, isn't she?"

Anger boiled in him, but he kept his face stony. "Yes, I suppose."

"You suppose? Come on, you would have to be a fool not to notice." He looked her up and down, and a cruel smile formed. "What I wouldn't give to have my hands on that body."

"So you could do what you did to Emily?"

"Emily?" he looked up for a moment, as if trying to recall the name. He then laughed. "Oh, the blonde girl from a couple of weeks ago? Yes. Something quite like that."

Logan thought back to that day he'd seen Sallos outside the daycare. He had been so at ease as he placed his hand on his back and walked him forward.

"It is great to see you, my old friend," he had said. "Tell me, how are your current conquests going?"

"They are splendid," Sallos replied with a satisfied smile. "In fact, that girl I was with Friday was one of them."

"Oh?"

"Yes." He chuckled coldly. "Oh, how she screamed."

Logan did not particularly care what happened to her, but he would engage in the formalities.

"Tell me about it."

Sallos turned towards him, his eyes gleaming. "Perhaps I should show you."

He gestured towards him, leading them to a black Cadillac parked against the curb. He opened the car door, without even sticking in a key, revved the engine to life. Logan got in the front seat next him, relishing the vehicle's luxury.

"Is this your car?" Logan asked.

Sallos gave a small smirk. "It is now."

He put the Cadillac into drive and sped onto the street, pulling in front of a line of cars.

"You bring too much attention to yourself, Sallos," Logan said distastefully.

"And you don't bring enough. Honestly, why should beings like us hide?"

He raced through a light just as it turned red, nearly striking the side of a silver van. The driver shot him the middle finger.

"Because there are *rules*. Every being has them, even ones like us."

"Rules are meant to be broken."

"Not the Master's."

He sighed as he slowed the car to the speed limit. They were obviously nearing their destination.

"I haven't broken any rules. Do I push the limits of said rules? Yes. But I have never broken them."

"Be sure that you don't." He looked around as the car continued to slow. "And where are you taking me, anyways? You don't still have her, do you?"

"Like I said, I'm going to show you."

They pulled into an abandoned school building. It was shabby and dark, with graffiti extending up the side, and dusty windows displaying large cracks. The brick on the outside was old and crusted, and the front double doors had peeling white paint.

He raised his eyebrows at Sallos. "An abandoned elementary school?"

He grinned. "Come on."

They got out of the car and traveled up the dirty steps. The fragile white doors were held together by a chain, but Sallos snapped the lock with ease and pulled them open, revealing empty hallways riddled with garbage.

"I dosed her with chloroform as soon as she stepped into the car," he began. "And then I carried her in here . . ."

Logan followed him through the halls, old leaves crunching beneath his feet. They turned and trailed through a dark hallway, the only light coming in from evenly spaced out windows. Sallos' pace quickened as the neared the end of the hall. A big smile formed on his face as he stopped at the last room on the left. He peered at Logan, his shoulders arched back with pride.

"In here."

Logan was only mildly curious. He stepped past Sallos and into the old classroom. He looked down, and took a step back.

It was Emily . . . or at least, what was left of her. Her mutilated body was sprawled across the concrete floor. Her pale face was riddled with bruises and scratches, an upside-down cross carved into her forehead. Her hands had been cut off as well as her feet, and a large bloody wound marked the side of her naked body, extending from beneath her chest all the way down to her hip. Her arms and her genitals were characterized by big, black bruises- he must have violated her beforehand. Her cold, dead eyes stared at the ceiling, her mouth still half open with horror.

He never would have guessed this was the same girl.

Logan wasn't sure what to say as his friend stepped up next to him. "Do you like it?"

"Did you do all of this before you killed her?"

Sallos chuckled. "What do you think?"

". . . It is certainly a fine piece of work. But perhaps I could appreciate it more if it were done properly."

He frowned. "What do you mean?"

"Honestly, you should know better than this," he said sternly. "How long has this body been in here? Three days now?"

"Oh, come on. No one even comes near to this building. It won't be found for a while."

"Still, you *know* you are supposed to dispose of your bodies! This is really careless, Sallos."

He shook his head and sighed, making a tsk tsk noise on the tip of his tongue. "You see, this is why you're not invited to parties, Logan. You're such a buzzkill."

"Logan?"

He looked up suddenly. "Yes?"

"You spaced out on me," Sallos said with a smile.

"Did I? Sorry about that." He looked back at the stage, where Marianne was just walking off the side. His shoulders sunk in disappointment. He had hoped to hear the whole audition. Of course Sallos had to come in and ruin everything. A new girl with a big white teeth came on the stage. He ignored her and turned towards his old friend.

"What are you doing here, anyways?"

"Oh, I just came to see how *your* conquest is going. How is the girl coming along?"

"She's doing great. Just a few more days and I'm sure to have a signature."

"Hmm, I see. And does she know about the little catch to your deal?"

Logan paused. "What have you heard, Sallos?"

"Oh nothing, nothing. Just that you've been after this girl for over two weeks and haven't told her the full details of the proposal. Oh, and I also heard that you spent a whole day with her, no discussion of business; just *hanging out*. Now, I said that that wasn't possible, of course. Not the one who just scolded *me* for bending the rules. Was I right to defend you, Logan?"

He sighed and turned around. "I guess news travels quickly down there," he muttered.

Sallos' face went stony. "What do you think you're doing?"

"I'm biding my time," Logan said a little too loudly. "I need this girl to trust me."

"She thinks you saved her life. How much more trust does she need?"

"I'm just making sure that the job gets done right."

"You've never done this with anyone else." A look of realization suddenly sparkled in his eyes. "Oh, don't tell me that this is actually Logan Lokte I am speaking to? Because I *know* that's not possible."

"What do you mean? You are speaking to both of us. We work together . . . we're a team."

A cruel smile formed on Sallos' face. "Only the real Logan would believe something so foolish."

He suddenly began circling him like a shark around its prey. Logan held his ground, determined not to break his gaze.

"Tell me. How long you been rising to the surface of that pathetic body?"

"I don't know what you're talking about," Logan said. "He is still inside me."

"Oh yes, but been quiet lately, has he? Been having some arguments with him?"

He did not know how to respond. He just peered silently into those dead eyes.

"You have feelings for the girl."

He started to protest, but Sallos put his index finger into the air. "That wasn't a question. I know you do. I can smell her all over you. But you listen to me very carefully. You go back into your little hole and forget all about Marianne Garcia. Let him take over the rest; he will close the deal much better than you could ever hope to. Give up and go back. You signed a contract four years ago, Logan. You had best honor it."

"And if I don't?"

Sallos smiled. "Well then the Master will not be too pleased with you. To hear that you haven't been doing your job? And you wouldn't be the only one punished, I'm sure. The girl would probably be put to some use."

Fury rose up within him.

"Hmmm. Maybe I could have a spin with her. Like what I did to Emily, right?"

Logan wanted nothing more than to attack him right then and there. Instead, he replied as evenly and calmly as possible.

"Don't worry. I will do my job."

Sallos peered at him for a moment before backing away slowly, his smile not matching his cold leer. "See that you do."

Chapter 8

"And so then I said, 'Mom. You can't be serious!' And she was like, 'Oh yeah. He ran out of there like a jackrabbit.'"

Logan laughed as Marianne finished the end of her story. They were gathered in the living room of her apartment, a bottle of wine sitting on the coffee table and two full glasses held in their hands. It was a red merlot that shined as the setting sun sent purple rays of light into the room. He had been planning to tell her about the deal, but he had already been there two hours, and he still had not found the proper moment to do it.

"Your mom sounds hilarious," he said while taking a sip of his drink.

"Yeah, she is. I love her to death." The implication of the phrase seemed to dawn on her after she said it, and her face sunk for a moment. Logan began to offer words of comfort when she suddenly perked up. "So, Mr. Logan Lokte, I seem to be doing all the talking here. What about you? What's your story?"

He frowned. The last thing he wanted was for her to know *his* story.

"I don't have one," he replied, sinking back in his chair.

"Oh come on, you've got to give me something. I mean, we've known each other for almost three weeks, and I barely know anything about you."

"You know stuff about me."

"Oh, sure. I know that you are a hero, and that there is something in your past you're running from. I know that you have some type of powers . . ."

"And that I am devilishly handsome," he finished her sentence.

She grinned. "That too. But seriously, what about real stuff? Like, what are your hobbies? What do you like to do?"

He had to think about this. He hadn't had any real hobbies for almost four years. What did he do before?

"I . . . I like building things."

She tilted her head curiously. "Building things? Like what?"

"Anything. I like putting things together, fixing them, solving problems. I used to want to be an architect." The words felt strange on his tongue. It was an old dream, a dream that had faded long ago, along with his life . . .

"Used to?" she inquired. "You don't want to anymore?"

". . . I finished my bachelor's degree in architecture. But circumstances got in the way of me continuing my education."

He said no more on the subject.

". . . So you couldn't be an architect. That's okay. What about the little stuff? Like, what's your favorite color?"

He raised his eyebrows. "You want to know my favorite color?"

"Yup."

"Okay . . ." Again, he had to search his memory. "I suppose it would be green."

She nodded as if she were considering this. "Mine is blue."

"Like the ocean?"

"No, like the sky. Stable. Unchanging."

"Unless there's a tornado."

She laughed at the unexpected comment. "Yes, unless there's that."

He chuckled to himself. He could feel the force inside him getting impatient; *bring up the deal already,* it said. *If you value both of your lives . . .*

Would you shut up? Logan said. *I know what I'm doing.*

It growled lowly in his ear.

"Okay, what else can I ask you?" She peered ahead thoughtfully. "How about family? Do you have family?"

"Some. My mother and father live in the city, and I have one set of grandparents that live in New Jersey."

"Oh that's nice! But you don't get to see them often?"

He looked down at the laminate floors. "No. Not much at all, actually. They probably wouldn't appreciate the person I am now."

"Well, surely there's someone you'd be willing to go see. Someone in your life who could appreciate you as you are?"

"Besides you?"

Her cheeks flushed red. He gazed towards the window, peering out at the dingy buildings reflected by orange-purple light.

"There was someone who could."

". . . A girl?"

He nodded slowly. "She died."

Marianne looked upon his grief-ridden face, pity melting her heart. "I'm sorry."

He sighed and shook his head. "It was a long time ago. Anyways, forgive me, I'm bringing down the mood. What kind of music do you enjoy, Marianne?"

"Oh, well, I enjoy most music. I guess my favorites would be show tunes and jazz."

"Always good."

"How about you?"

"70's rock."

"The 70's was definitely the best era for rock," she replied with a smile.

"See? You understand me."

She laughed and took a sip of her merlot, which was now a tiny puddle at the bottom of her glass. "Favorite food?"

"Italian, definitely."

"Mine too. How about your favorite drinks?"

"Alcoholic ones? Whiskey and soda, or red wine."

"Good choices. Mine is champagne. Speaking of drinks, are you ready for a night of cocktails and free food this Friday?"

"You mean the actor's banquet? You know I am. Every night spent with you is a great one."

She gazed up slowly from her glass. They looked at each other for a long moment, their dark eyes sending silent signals like a stream of electricity.

". . . Even when you do interrogate me with questions."

She hit him playfully on the arm and they chuckled, their laughter sounding out into the expanse of the night.

~~~

Logan left the apartment in good spirits.

They had talked until one a.m., until Marianne finally toppled on her bed. He made sure her alarm was set, placed the covers over her, and left, strolling down the stairs and out under the night sky. He felt closer to her than ever. He had not shared that much with another person in a long time. It was refreshing, like releasing a huge load that had been pressing on his chest. Despite the bitterness brewing from the thing inside him, he exited the building with a smile.

Almost as soon as he stepped outside, a figure emerged from the shadows of a nearby alleyway.

"Well that went well, didn't it?"

He sighed as he turned to face Sallos. His blonde hair was slicked back, his blue eyes seeming even more menacing than usual in the moonlight.

"You know, your stalking is getting old," Logan said irritably. "Would you mind stepping back and letting me do my job?"

"Oh, your job? Is that what you were doing? Because it seemed to me that you were discussing your favorite colors."

"Go away, Sallos."

He started walking forward, when he felt Sallos' hand clasp his shoulder.

"Our Master knows about your little rebellious streak," he whispered.

Cold chills traveled down Logan's spine.

"Well you can tell the Master that I have things under control."

"I don't think you do. If you did, I wouldn't have been sent to watch you."

Logan was taken aback. "You?"

"I may bend the rules, but at least I am loyal to our Master. Where do *your* loyalties lie?"

He tried to escape again, but found his path blocked by Sallos. "You signed a contract, Logan Lokte," he said, his voice rising. "A lifetime of servitude to Satan. You would share your body with a demon, and in return, Lucifer would help you get the revenge you so desperately wanted. You got your revenge. Now you hold up your end of the bargain."

"I have served."

"For four years? Hardly a lifetime!"

"I'm not rebelling, and I'm not going to screw this up. I know what I'm doing. All that matters is that she signs, right? Well, she will. I guarantee it."

Sallos raised his eyebrows. "You are going to propose the deal to her this Friday at the banquet. You are going to tell her everything, and you are going to get her to sign."

Logan's breath became unsteady as fear began to take hold. Fear. Such an old, weak emotion.

". . . I can't do all that in one night."

Sallos smirked and leaned towards him, his lips nearly touching Logan's ear. "If you don't tell her, I will."

He closed his eyes, and when he opened them, Sallos was gone.

Chapter 9

Marianne stared in the oval shaped mirror. She looked pale for someone with naturally dark skin. The nightmares must have been taking a toll.

She held her hair up around her cheeks. She let it down. Up, down, up, down. She couldn't decide. And her makeup? How was she going to hide the dark circles beneath her eyes? She would have to use the eye brightener that was tucked in the back shelf under her sink. Yes, that would do the trick.

Marianne had always been good at applying makeup. She didn't know why. She remembered the first time she put on makeup by herself. She was twelve, and the assorted colors laid before like an artist's pallet. Colored eye shadows, eyeliner, face powder, three different lip sticks, rosy pink blush, volume mascara; it was all there for her to play with. Sure that her mom wasn't watching, she painted her canvas with excitement. Soon that plain, dull face turned into a masterpiece. Dark red lips, pink cheeks, sparkly eye shadow with thick, winged eyeliner. She never knew she could look that pretty.

Now that she was older, Marianne understood the vanity involved in a woman's expectation to wear makeup. Yet, she couldn't seem to break the habit. It was an addiction she had no desire to stop.

Up. She definitely wanted to wear her hair up.

Just as she was about to stick in the first bobby pin, her cell phone began vibrating next to her. She held the phone to her ear while putting up her hair.

"Hi sweetheart."

"Hey Mom," she grunted. The pin was not wanting to stick. "How are you?"

"Oh, fine I guess. Just trying to search through these stupid channels. Hospital cable never has anything to watch."

"Probably because the only things you watch are crime dramas."

"Well, they need more of those."

She smiled. "Want me to complain to the hospital for you?"

"No, no, it's alright. I get released in a few days anyways."

Marianne's eyes went wide as she dropped her case of pins on the floor. They sprawled in different directions on the tile.

"You're getting released?" she asked, exasperated. "That's great!"

"Yes, I just hope I don't have to come back to this place anytime soon. You know I hate hospitals."

She frowned. "I know . . ."

"I mean, white walls? Bad food? No good channels? It's like they try to make me uncomfortable here."

"At least you'll be back in a few days."

"That's what I'm hoping. It'd be nice to be in my own bed again. But anyways, how are you, girl? How are things working out with your hero?"

She couldn't help but smile. "I'm pretty good. Emily still hasn't turned up, but Logan really helps me feel better about it."

"You think this is the guy for you?" She sounded excited.

"Mom, I've only known him for three weeks . . ."

"It took me that long to fall in love with your father! Well, I guess that's a bad example. Hopefully your hero wouldn't run out on you as soon as he found out you were pregnant . . ."

"He wouldn't. I mean, not that I'm planning on getting pregnant or anything."

"But baby, you know if you did, I'd be here to support you!"

Marianne felt her face turn red. "Mom . . ."

"You don't have to be scared to tell me anything, okay? I'll always be here, no matter what trouble you get into."

She shook her head. "I know, thank you."

"So when are you going to see that boy again?"

She sighed with satisfaction as she successfully pinned up her hair. "Actually tonight. He's my date to the actor's banquet."

"Oh! Well look at you!"

"I know. There's just something about him. I don't know what it is, but I've never felt so myself around anyone. I think I really, really like him." Hearing it aloud, she realized how true it was.

"What about that deal he wanted to make with you?"

Marianne paused. She had not updated her mother on that. After all, what would she say? That he had powers? She would think Mari was crazy.

"I don't know," she lied. "He hasn't mentioned it."

"Well girl, you both are in my prayers. I pray for you every night, you know."

She felt a stab of guilt dig into her stomach. ". . . Thank you."

"I'll probably let you go though so you can get ready for your party. I just wanted to call and see how you were doing."

"Alright, I appreciate it, Mom. I love you."

(68)

"I love you too, honey; with all my heart. I'll talk to you later."
"Alright, bye."
"Goodbye."
The phone hung up with a swift click.

~~~

Logan buttoned the tuxedo nervously, forcing the tight jacket over his broad shoulders.

He was anxious about the banquet. What Sallos had said was tickling the back of his mind like a pestering fly. *If you don't tell her, I will . . .* Of course, that meant Logan would have to tell her tonight. But how? Even in his most determined moments, she tended to melt his resolve into a miniscule puddle. The voice inside him was not helping.

You heard what Sallos said, it said. *If you insist on going to this silly party, you must use it to propose the offer. Get a few drinks in her if you must; just get her to sign the contract. Lucifer is watching us now. We must not fail.*

I know, I know, Logan replied irritably. He wished his other half would shut up and let him think. It was becoming a nuisance, having his thoughts heard all the time. Before their thoughts seemed one and the same, but now it was like a constant monitor on his mind that he was unable to get away from.

There was one other reason he was nervous about tonight, a reason he barely wanted to admit to himself. This was his first official date with Marianne.

He sprayed on some cologne and squeezed a glob of gel into his hand. Slicked back hair? Or styled messy? Maybe a mix of both?

His first real date would be spent telling Marianne he was half-demon. Yes, that would go over well. He could just picture it: "Hi Marianne!" he would say. "Nice dress. By the way, I'm working for the devil, and I'm sharing my body with a demon from hell. I was wondering if you wanted to do the same?" He couldn't do all of this in one night. Impress Marianne, while still telling her the truth and getting her to sign the contract? It was just too much.

So focus on the latter, the demon hissed.

I didn't ask you.

If your wretched feelings ruin this for us . . .

Shut up. I've got it.

He placed a frazzled hand over his ear. He wanted to be excited. He loved being with Marianne. He could not understand what it was about her that was so drawing, but he knew that he wanted to be with her, and perhaps the best way to do that was to get her to sign the contract. Then his Master may let them be together.

His fingers fumbled over his black tie. Thirty minutes. In thirty minutes, he would have to figure out how to propose a deal with Satan, explain that he lied to her, and still maintain her affections. That couldn't be too hard . . . right?

Chapter 10

Logan knocked on Marianne's door for the third time, a red rose clutched in his sweaty hand. It felt like he'd been there for hours, and his nerves were increasing every second.

"Coming!" her voice echoed through the door.

He wished she would hurry. He had been preparing all day, and he wanted to get the night underway. The demon was anxious too. He could feel it within him, impatiently waiting for the conversation to take place . . .

The door flew open.

Marianne appeared like an angel. She wore a long, yellow chiffon gown with a halter top embedded with a million tiny rhinestones, and on her neck she donned beautiful jewels that sparkled in the fluorescent light. Her makeup was perfectly polished, her lips showcasing a glossy shine. Her eyes came at a long wing on each side, her lids like sparkling silver. Finally, there was her hair, which was pulled up into a styled bun with long ringlets cascading down her shoulders. She looked stunning.

"Marianne . . ." His mouth hung open. "You're beautiful."

She flashed a dazzling smile. "Thank you. You look great too!"

He suddenly remembered the rose in his hand. He held it up to her. "For the lady."

She took the flower and put it up to her nose, inhaling the fresh scent. "How sweet. Thank you."

"My pleasure." He held out his arm. She smiled and grabbed onto it, allowing him to lead her down the stairs and to the cab that waited outside.

They arrived at the venue in fifteen minutes. The banquet was taking place at a large hotel in Manhattan, the outside shaped from white stone that ascended into the sky in a splendid array of Gothic architecture. They entered through the two big glass doors and walked into the lobby. The lobby floors were made of marble, its high vaulted ceilings showcasing an enormous chandelier adorned with sparkling crystals that twinkled like stars.

They were directed to the back ballroom. When they went inside, Marianne felt her breath catch in her throat. Chandeliers- several of them, lining the ornately painted ceiling. The floor there was also made of marble, and the walls were characterized by large, arching windows that overlooked the New York City skyline. There were rows upon rows of circular tables decorated with large, floral centerpieces, and taking up the whole middle of the room was an enormous dance floor that shined like glass. Dozens of waiters holding huge silver trays, sparkling cloth stretched across every table, walls painted gold. Hundreds of people gathered, all dressed like movie stars.

Logan looked at her half-open mouth and smiled. This was obviously a new experience for her. He was proud to be the one to share it with her.

They walked through the ballroom, weaving around people until they made their way to a table. Just as they were about to a sit, a voice called out behind them:

"Marianne Garcia!"

They turned around, and Marianne smiled. A large dark-skinned man stood before them, with short silver gray hair and a tuxedo that was too small for his protruding stomach. He held out his arms welcomingly.

"Marianne, one of my favorite actresses!"

"Hello, Chris."

He clasped onto her wrist, both hands cupped over hers. "I must say Mari, you look ravishing tonight."

"Well thank you." She peered over at Logan. "Logan, this is my agent, Christopher Ballard. Chris, this is Logan."

He reached for Logan's hand and shook it rapidly. "Great to meet you Logan! This is my wife, Leslie." He motioned to the woman standing behind him. She was stick thin with straight black hair that went down to her waist.

Logan smiled cordially. "It's very nice to meet you."

She acknowledged his comment with a nod.

"So how are you liking the party?" Chris asked.

Marianne replied, "Well we actually just got here, but we love it so far. It's truly breathtaking."

"Yeah, the Actor's Guild spared no expense tonight. Speaking of which, how would you like to meet some Broadway producers?"

She gazed at Logan uncertainly before looking back at her agent. "That . . . that sounds lovely."

They followed Chris through hoards of people, Marianne grasping onto Logan's arm. They eventually reached a couple a few tables down, and Chris tapped on the woman's shoulder lightly.

She whipped around. She was tall and stern-faced, with shoulder-length auburn hair and wrinkles lining her mouth and eyes.

She donned a long-sleeved black dress with cascading ruffles that reached the floor. Despite her narrow, critical eyes, she smiled.

"Christopher Ballard."

"Alexa Hopkins! It's been too long."

"Yes, yes it has. I would like you to meet my husband Rick."

All eyes trailed to the man standing beside her. He was fairly plain looking; tall, with blue eyes and gray hair. He smiled and offered his hand.

"Pleasure to meet you, Chris."

They went through another formal introduction, after which he practically shoved Marianne forward. "And this is one of my clients, Marianne Garcia."

They nodded in her direction. "How do you do, Marianne?"

She smiled nervously and offered a nod. "Pleasure."

"She moved here from Kansas a few years ago," Chris continued. "She's an underdog with a lot of talent."

"Really?" Alexa inquired. "Well, it just turns out, I am producing a Broadway musical that would be perfect for you, Marianne."

"Are you serious?"

"Yes! You are beautiful, skinny; you have the perfect look for one of our chorus girls. I'd love for you to come to our auditions in two weeks."

Marianne was in awe. "That . . . that would be great! Thank you!"

"Your welcome. Just remind me when you get there that we met at the banquet. I will make sure to give you special consideration."

After they left the couples, Marianne was in high spirits.

"Can you believe it?" she said to Logan. "She personally asked me to audition for her!"

"I know. That's great."

"Of course, it's in only two weeks, so I'm going to have to hurry and get something prepared. What should I perform? I guess I don't have to decide tonight. I'm just so excited. I've never had an acting connection before!"

Seeing her happy made him feel alight. But how was he going to tell her about the deal now? He couldn't bear to break that innocent enthusiasm . . .

They made their way back to their large circular table. The gold tablecloth sparkled, and the rose centerpiece gave off a sweet, fresh smell that reminded Logan of a garden. There were eight other people at their table, but all they could see was each other.

"This place is so amazing!" Marianne mused, taking a sip of champagne. "I always wanted to live in Manhattan."

"Don't we all?"

"Yeah, but then I looked at the prices for apartments."

Logan laughed. "Didn't have five thousand a month to pay for one of those?"

"Working at a daycare? Sadly out of my budget."

This seemed like a good opportunity to bring up the benefits of the deal. But the words never came.

"Well, when you become a famous actress on Broadway . . ."

"I doubt that will happen," she interjected.

". . . As I was saying, *when* you become a famous actress on Broadway, you will be able afford one."

"You can too, if you ever decide to go back and become a brilliant architect."

He frowned while thinking about his old dream. "I very much doubt that will happen."

"Well, you never know. Life may surprise you."

He gazed at Marianne, her smooth caramel skin, dark waves, intense milky eyes; he suddenly realized that she was perfect. Everything about her, all the good, all the bad. She was perfect.

". . . I think it already has."

She smiled kindly and put a tender hand on his. "You're such a good man, Logan."

He wanted to laugh, but his voice came out in a whisper. ". . . No. I'm not."

"You are. If only you could see what I see. You are wonderful."

For once the demon was silent within him, and he felt himself, his true self, longing to tell her everything.

To explain what a mistake it was to trust him.

". . . Marianne, I need to tell you something."

She gazed up at him, her eyes like orbs. "Yes?"

His heart pounded hard in his chest. Sweat formed on the back of his neck. That old, horrible fear began to take root. In a single moment, he knew he couldn't tell her.

"Well, I was actually, um, wondering if you'd . . . like to dance?"

She blinked in surprise. "Really? Isn't the song almost over?"

She was right. The slow, romantic ballad playing in the background was nearly at an end, and the couples were already beginning to disperse.

"Well, you can't blame a man for trying," he said with a forced smile.

"No, no wait, I'm sorry. Let's try this again. Logan Lokte, I would love to dance with you."

They stood up slowly, her hand in his, and traveled to the dance floor. They found their spot in the middle of the marble floor. Logan slid his hands to her waist. She placed hers on his shoulders.

The demon brewed with anger.

They were so close. Their faces were only inches apart. They began to sway back and forth, taking small, light steps on each side.

But before they could really begin, the song stopped. They stood awkwardly as they waited for the next song to start.

It began after a moment of silence, a slow, beautiful start that, after a few seconds, turned into an upbeat jazz song. Though it was fast paced, it had a sensuality to it that brought couples back on the floor. Marianne and Logan exchanged questioning looks, telepathically asking the other if they should continue.

"Do you know how to dance to this?" he finally inquired.

"I majored in Acting; I took a million dance classes. I think the question is, do *you* know how to dance to this?"

He grabbed her waist, his free hand sliding into hers. She giggled as they started to move to the beat, forming synchronized steps across the floor.

"And where did you learn to dance?" she asked.

"I'll have you know I was a dedicated member of Ballroom Dancing Club in college."

"Is that so?"

"Oh yes. I was voted best male dancer."

"Only a real man would admit that."

". . . I'll take that as a compliment."

She laughed as he spun her around, her dress whipping in the air. Their hips swayed each way, their palms clasped together. Marianne could feel his hand clutched firmly around her waist. Her tiny hand was placed softly on his shoulder, and he longed to feel that hand move, to travel lightly down to his chest. They were so close. Their bodies moved perfectly to the jazzy beat. He spun her around, brought her back in. Their eyes met. They could not seem to peel their gaze from one another. The music rose.

Suddenly, there was no one else there. All the surrounding bodies seemed to dissolve in a blurry whirl. The music rose again. The moves became more fast-paced, the steps bringing them closer. Logan couldn't even hear the demon. All he could focus on was her.

Trumpets blared as the music neared its big finish. Two more twirls, Marianne soaring tightly into him, so close that their faces were only centimeters apart. Before he realized what he was doing, he leaned in and kissed her.

Their lips met in a slow and passionate embrace as the song played its last notes. They lingered softly for a moment, parted, then came in again. They clung soundlessly together, neither wanting the moment to end.

Finally they separated, and their eyes met before Logan leaned in, delivering a gentle kiss on her forehead. He held her in a sweet embrace until the next song began. They then made their way off of the dance floor, ending up at a nearby table filled with food and punch.

Neither was sure what to say to the other. How could it be expressed in words?

". . . Would you like some punch or anything?" he asked tentatively.

"I might in a minute. Thanks."

A sharp, piercing sound struck Logan's ear drum. He clutched his ear tightly, the frequency so high that it made his head throb. There were words being said too, but they were being repeated too quickly to understand. He forced a teeth-grinding smile and looked at Marianne.

"I have to go to the bathroom."

"Oh, okay." She seemed disappointed by this. He gave her a quick kiss on he cheek. "I won't be long."

Marianne watched as he made his way through the sea of golden tables and out of sight. She then looked forward and leaned on the table, the dance from moments ago repeating in her memory. She smiled.

"Excuse me, are you Marianne Garcia?"

She turned around. A well-dressed man with blonde hair was standing behind her, his blue eyes sharp.

"Yes. Who you are you?"

A smile formed on the corner of his lips. "Forgive me, where are my manners? My name is Sallos."

Logan pushed his way to the other end of the ballroom. The ringing was deafening. He forced his way out of the doors and into the hallway, where he leaned against the outer wall.

STOP! He hoped he hadn't said that aloud.

How many chances have you had tonight?! You have failed. I am taking over.

No! I won't let you.

Why are you making this so difficult? You only had one job, Logan: get her to sign the contract. After three weeks, she doesn't even know what the contract is! You are done.

No, I'm not. I'll go and tell her now.

You couldn't tell her minutes ago. What makes this time any different?

I will. If you would just let me, I will go and tell her this second.

The demon paused. *You will tell her.*

I will.

. . . Because if you don't, you know what consequences lie for us both.

. . . I know.

"Sallos?" she mused. "What an interesting name."

"Yes, it is. And might I say Marianne, you are an absolute enchantment tonight."

". . . Thank you," she replied slowly. His eyes were trailing her body with a hunger that made her shift with discomfort. "I'm sorry, but do I know you from somewhere? You look awfully familiar."

"Well, I do have one of those faces. But as it happens, we actually have some acquaintances in common. I believe one of them is your date tonight."

"Oh, you know Logan?"

He flashed a devilish smile. "Oh yes. We go way back." He took a sudden step forward. She found herself backing up. "Mr. Lokte has grown quite fond of you, hasn't he?"

". . . I don't know," she hesitated. "What has he told you?"

"Just that you two are close. He cares about you. Not that I can blame him for wanting you. Even I want you. You, Marianne, have a body that angels lust for."

He continued to survey her chest down to her hips. She longed to change the subject.

"You said, acquaintances?"

He leaned back, resting his arm on the table. "Yes. I have also had the pleasure of meeting one of your coworkers. Emily, I think was her name."

She perked up. "You know Emily?!"

"Yes. A very nice girl."

". . . Well then you'll know then that she is missing. She hasn't been seen for three weeks."

He rubbed his chin thoughtfully. "Three weeks? Well, that can't be right. In fact, I just saw her around two weeks ago."

"You saw her? Where is she? Is she okay?!"

He reached into his slacks and dug out a sleek, black phone. He held it up tauntingly. "Would you like to see for yourself?"

~~~

Logan walked back into the ballroom, weaving through the crowd. This was it. He was going to tell her everything. The thought sent painful nausea to his stomach, but he would have to work through it this time. He had no choice.

Peering beyond the flocks of people, he saw Marianne talking to someone. At first, he figured she must have ran into someone she knew. But as he studied that tall, muscular frame, a cold shiver trickled down his back.

Sallos.

His slow, steady pace turned into a run. He didn't care about the questioning eyes of the people he was pushing past. He had to get to her. He could see Sallos more clearly now, holding a phone out to Marianne. She was reaching for it . . .

He jumped between the two of them, his chest heaving.

"Logan what are you doing?!" Marianne asked incredulously.

"Yes, Logan, what are you doing?" Sallos portrayed mock innocence.

"Marianne, get away from him."

"What? Logan, he's seen Emily. He was just about to show me a picture of her . . ."

Logan held his arm in front of her. "No!"

She placed a hand on her hip and raised her eyebrows. "Why not?"

"Just don't, please. This man cannot be trusted."

Sallos shrugged his shoulders up. "What a way to treat an old friend! You would know how Emily is doing, Logan. You were with me when we saw her."

Marianne turned towards Logan. "You *saw* her? How could you not tell me?"

"Yes Logan, how could you not tell her?"

"Shut up!" He placed a gentle hand on her shoulder. "Mari, please. You don't want to see her."

"Why not?!"

A crowd was beginning to develop around them.

"Why don't you step aside and let your kitten have a peek?" Sallos said.

"I'm sorry, his what?"

"No," he said, shaking his head rapidly.

"Oh, for goodness sake." Marianne grabbed Logan's arm and shoved him to the side. She pulled the screen to her face- and let it fall to the ground. She doubled over and wretched, one hand supported on the table.

Logan could see the picture from where he was standing. It was a picture of Emily just as he had seen her before; naked, bruises scattered across her legs and genitals, her hands and feet cut off, nothing but bloody stubs.

Sallos laughed hysterically. "She's had better days!"

Logan was unsure of what to do. He reached out for her. "Marianne . . ."

"Don't touch me! You . . . you knew about this! You knew she was . . . she was . . ."

"Cut up into little pieces?" Sallos offered.

Marianne ran forward, her nostrils flared and her skin flushing a bright red. Logan held her in place as she thrashed wildly.

"YOU'RE DISGUSTING! YOU ARE SICK! WHAT HAVE YOU DONE TO HER?!"

"Marianne! Marianne stop!" Logan cried. "Stop, Mari! He'll kill you!"

Sallos continued to laugh as she threw herself against Logan's arms. He was finding it increasing difficult to keep her still.

"Mari . . ."

She only fought harder. She reached up her arm, scratching his shoulder . . .

"MARIANNE, STOP!"

In a sudden passion, he shoved her against the table. Her arm flung against the punch bowl. It toppled onto the cloth, the red liquid flying all over her dress. The soft yellow was now drenched in dark red, the punch dripping down her legs and onto the marble.

Surprised waiters hurried to clean up the spill. Logan gazed at her defaced form with wide eyes.

"Marianne . . . I'm so sorry . . ."

"Stop." She said dangerously. "You said if you couldn't convince me in three weeks, I would never have to see you again. Well your three weeks are up, Logan Lokte. My answer is no."

She stormed off, her body rigid as she stomped through the ballroom, past the gawking crowd, and out the double doors. Logan's heart felt as if it were about to explode.

Sallos' chuckle echoed behind him. "Touchy, much?"

He whipped to face him. He boiled with anger as he looked at Sallos' wretched smirk.

"Really, Logan. You must learn to control your woman."

He marched up to the demon until they were only a foot from each other. "Why would you do that?!"

Sallos shrugged. "I was just doing your job."

"My job? My job was to get her to make the deal, not show her pictures of her dead friend!"

The crowd of shocked faces was getting thicker around them.

"I admit my methods were unorthodox. But at least I got closer than you did. You were too busy trying to sleep with the whore to accomplish anything worthwhile."

He thrusts his hands against Sallos' chest. Sallos stumbled, then responded with a hard smack that sent Logan flying to the floor. Security officers rallied to reprimand Sallos, but the demon grabbed each of them by the head, twisting them completely around. Their necks snapped in an instant, and the bodies toppled onto the marble.

The people were in terror. Many of them attempted to bolt towards the exit, but with a flick of Sallos' hand the doors shut tight, locked by an unseen force. Everyone backed away and huddled towards the edges of the room.

"What do you expect?" he continued with a dramatic gesture of his arms. "I am Sallos! The demon of chaos! You want me to be subtle, Logan?"

He reached out and grabbed a nearby woman in a red dress, holding her by the neck. She whimpered, her face contorted with fear.

"Would you prefer me to subtly kill this woman?"

He sniffed her neck like a predator sniffing its meal. She screamed.

Logan held his hands up. "Don't. Just remember the rules, Sallos. You are making a scene."

"Remember the rules?" he repeated with a high-pitched laugh. "How many rules have you broken? I'm not even sure the rules matter anymore!" His eyes searched the fearful crowd. "I could kill all of you right now!"

Fearful cries erupted.

"And I think I will. Starting with this one."

He held up his hand, preparing to smash it down on the woman's face. Logan was frozen. He waited to hear her screams diminish into cold, dead silence.

"No. You won't."

They turned to the unseen voice. A woman marched towards them from the side, her heels clicking against the marble floor, her hips swaying back and forth. She had long, fiery red hair that stretched down her back. Her eyes were painted with thick black eye liner, her lips shining a sharp, bright red. The black dress hugged her curvy body.

The civilians in the room did not know who this woman was. But Logan and Sallos did. They could sense it, the terrible power that radiated off of her feminine figure.

This was Lucifer.

She glided towards them, her hands pressed to her side. They fell on their knees before her. The woman who had been in Sallos' grasp stumbled up, her rickety crawl turning into a full run back to the crowd.

"Master," Sallos began. "I didn't know you would be here . . ."

"Spare the speech, Sallos. Both of you. On your feet."

They staggered upward. She flashed a short, polite smile. "Now, boys. Let's have a little talk in my office, shall we?"

She grabbed onto their sleeves, and in an instant, they were gone.

Chapter 11

Marianne sat in her bed as her tea turned cold beside her. She gazed at the blue curtain that separated her bedroom from the rest of the apartment, her toes clenching at the scratchy sheets. What happened at the banquet echoed over and over in her mind. That horrible man and his chilling laughter, the picture of the defaced Emily lying dead on a dusty floor. And Logan. Of all people, Logan. He had known. He had known all along about Emily. He then had the nerve to kiss her! He actually dared to make Mari care about him. That was what hurt the most. More than anything, she felt betrayed.

    She took a sip of her chilled tea. She was all alone in this cursed city. Her only friend was dead, and her alleged more-than-a-friend seemed to have had a hand in it. She felt physically ill. It was like the whole world had been ripped from her, leaving her to suffer in this dark, damp hole of loneliness.

    You're not alone.

The voice within her mind sounded like a gentle echo. It was loving, calm. It was also incredibly familiar . . .

Was that God?

She reached in her nearby dresser and pulled out her bible. She skimmed through its thin pages, searching desperately for guidance. Finally she looked up, the popcorn ceiling staring down at her.

"Lord, please help me," she whispered. She had not prayed in a long time, and the words sounded strange to her own ears. "If you are there, if there still hope left for me, please tell me. Send me a sign. Anything will do. Just . . . just tell me what to do."

Tears began to fall down her cheeks. She wiped them away. She had cried enough already, and her face was starting to get raw.

At that moment her phone began to ring, flashing Christopher Ballard's number all over her screen.

She ignored it.

~~~

Logan plummeted for only a second before he was stopped by a hard, stony floor. He landed on his feet and looked ahead of him.

Nothing. He was in a room shrouded completely in darkness, the only light from a small fire suspended on a stone pillar. He could not see any walls or floor. All he could see was Sallos standing stiffly beside him, and Lucifer. She stood across from them, fire blazing in her black eyes.

Logan had not been surprised at the devil taking a woman's shape. All demons, including Satan, possessed no gender until they stepped inside a human body. But one thing was for certain as Logan peered into those two black holes; Lucifer was intimidating, no matter what the shape.

"Now," she started, her eyes trailing between the two of them. "As you both know, I am very busy, and I do not relish having to monitor my servants."

Sallos started: "We beg your forgiveness, great one . . ."

"You will speak when you are spoken to."

Sallos immediately went silent.

"Now, then, Sallos. I asked you to do one simple thing. I asked you to watch Logan, and see to it that he struck the deal in ample time. Instead, you scared the deal off, and attempted to slaughter a whole room of people, some of which haven't been won over yet."

Sallos stared at her with wide eyes. She pursed her lips impatiently. "You may speak now."

Sallos bowed his blonde head. "Forgive me, Master. I take full responsibility for my failure."

"Yes, I'm sure you do. Do not mistake me, Sallos. I admire your imagination and your lust for destruction, but you are reckless. Sometimes, you are a liability."

His mouth hung open fearfully. "If I may ask, your grace, what are you implying . . ?

She sneered. "Don't worry. I'll let you keep your precious body."

His shoulders sunk with relief.

". . . But since you have a body, why shouldn't I have fun with it? Six days in the Pit should teach you some respect."

Logan flinched. The Pit. The one thing all demons feared. Though he had never seen it, the Pit was supposedly a large, gaping hole, where one was forced to experience every type of pain, every ounce of suffering that existed on Earth. It was physical and mental. In one day a person could undergo grief, be set on fire, have every bone broken in their body, starve, experience self-loathing, abandonment, loneliness, childbirth . . . the list was endless. It was a fate worse than death.

Sallos was shaking. "My lord, do not, I beg you . . ."

Her face unchanging, she flicked her long, red nails at him. He cried out as his body began to disintegrate, slowly fading into nothingness.

She turned to Logan and smiled. "Now, where were we?"

He tried to hide the fear that penetrated his body. If the Pit was Sallos' punishment, what could she possibly have stored for him?

"Do not be afraid," she cooed, as if reading his thoughts. "Sallos was a demon, my servant by nature. He has to be made an example of. But I am not speaking to a demon right now, am I, Logan?"

Still tense, he shook his head.

"Yes. My little deceiver is buried deep beneath a pile of humanity. Not that I am surprised. You have a strong soul. It was only a matter of time before you attempted to regain control of your body."

Logan swallowed tentatively. "If you knew this would happen, why did you make the deal with me?"

She flashed a white grin. "Because you are strong. Strength is a valued asset here in the underworld. And you, paired with the great Liar; I knew the two of you would perform well together."

We did, he thought gravely.

". . . And you will."

He blinked in surprise. So she *was* reading his thoughts.

"Human or not, you signed a contract that binds you to me," she continued. "It is not one easily broken. I see that this girl has a hold on you, but you are to ignore it. You are to make no more advances on her. You will pursue no contact. In time, she will come to you and beg that you to let her sign. That, I will see to personally."

He wanted to ask how, but he didn't expect she would answer him.

"Now, as all this happens, things are going to go back to normal. You are to let the demon back in control so that you work as a team again. Is this all clear?"

He replied with a small nod. She trailed his body with her black eyes, a smirk forming at the corner of her mouth. "You have so much potential, Logan. Do not waste it on fleeting trifles."

"Understood."

". . . You had best not waste it. For both yours *and* Marianne's sake."

A cold chill crept through him as he stared into that cruel, blank face. He then felt his body surge upward. The pitch black of the room slowly turned to light as Logan's feet caught the rough concrete. His eyes had to adjust to the change of scenery.

He was back, standing on the streets of New York. Relief rushed over him like a tidal wave. He had never been so glad to see those tall, gray buildings. But his happiness was short lived, because one troublesome thought began to plague his mind, something he had not wondered in four years:

What now?

~~~

Logan looked out of the window of his hotel suite a week later, gazing blankly at the street below, the vertical structures twinkling in the distance. He had not heard from Marianne. Lucifer said he would, but he hadn't seen her since the banquet. He wished he had. He wished he could see her now, so he could apologize for everything that had happened . . .

Of course, what could an apology do? He had witnessed the mutilated body of her only friend, then kept it from her for over two weeks. His conscience had been like a wispy cloud before, but now he understood, fully and plainly; this was not something he could bounce back from, no matter how much he loved her. It was done.

Still, even with the knowledge that he may never get Marianne back, he couldn't bring himself to let the demon take control again. He couldn't stand the idea of not commanding his own thoughts. And Marianne . . . what would she be to him were the demon to be in control? When they first met, she meant nothing to him.

Now, she felt like his whole world.

Of course, there was a time when these feelings belonged to another. He frowned. Remembering her always brought on grief that ripped his insides.

He closed his eyes and tried to imagine her face. He had no pictures, and she was beginning to fade in his memory. It was amazing what the mind could forget without prolonged exposure.

Black hair. He remembered that clearly. It was silky smooth, like feathers on a dove's wing. A thin, petite body. Bright green eyes. A large, white smile that radiated warmth, even on the darkest of days. She was like an angel. He could still see her in that strapless white ball gown, walking down the aisle of the cathedral with her arm around her father's, her face beaming. In that moment, everything was surreal. He couldn't believe that, out of all the men in the world, she chose him. He couldn't believe he was marrying the woman of his dreams.

Jasmine . . . yes. Her name was Jasmine.

They had settled down quickly after they'd gotten married. They bought a little house outside the city, which they planned to renovate to make their dream home. Jasmine paid the bills working as a Medical Assistant while Logan finished up his bachelor's degree in Architecture. He smiled when he thought of those times. Marriage was hard, of course. They could end up fighting for hours if they weren't careful. But more hours were spent in each other's arms as they watched the sun set every night over the horizon. More were spent talking about their dreams, and what the big, mysterious future had in store for them.

They never could have guessed that their future held a child.

Their child. Conceived just as Logan was graduating college. He knew he couldn't pursue his Master's degree right away, not when Jasmine was pregnant. So they prepared. Logan got a paid internship at an architectural firm, and Jasmine continued her job. Sometimes they got so excited, they could hardly wait the nine months. They made all the preparations. They took parenting classes. They painted a nursery, and celebrated with a baby shower. They opted to know the gender- a girl- and named her Jennifer. Logan was so ready to meet her, to see that perfect mixture of chromosomes come to life in one little girl, to guide her through the big, wonderful world that they lived in. He could not wait to hold Jenny in his arms for the first time, then exchange a knowing smile with Jasmine, an image he knew would last forever in his memory.

But he never had the chance to meet her. Eight months into the pregnancy, Jasmine was hit by a drunk driver.

That day was like a blur. There were a bunch of technical terms being spewed out at him, things he couldn't comprehend.

One phrase, he did understand.

"I'm sorry, Mr. Lokte," the doctor said. "But your wife didn't make it."

That moment shattered his whole existence. It shook his faith in God . . . and it made him susceptible to Lucifer's advances.

By the time Satan reached him, Logan was already bent on enacting vengeance against the drunk driver that killed his wife and unborn child. He knew who the deal favored, but he didn't care. He had nothing more to lose. And that is when he began to share his body with the demon of deception. The "Great Liar," he was called. Together, they made an unstoppable team.

Until Marianne.

As Logan watched his breath form on the ten-story window, a knock sounded on the door of his hotel room. He jolted, then let out an aggravated sigh.

I swear, if that is housekeeping again...

He trudged over to the oak door and swung it open.

It wasn't housekeeping.

Marianne stood before him, her long hair drenched and her cheeks a puffy red. She wore a t-shirt with sweats, her eyes sparkling with determination. He considered the wet hair for a moment, then realized she must have just gotten out of the shower.

"M-Marianne!" His own voice was caught in his throat.

"Logan," she responded curtly.

"Look, about the banquet, I am so . . ."

"I don't want to talk about the banquet."

He blinked. ". . . Then why are you here?"

"For the deal," she said. "I want to make the deal."

Chapter 12

"You . . . you want to make the deal?"

"Yes, that's what I said."

He couldn't believe it. Just a week ago, she never wanted to see him again. Yet here she was now, wanting to strike the deal. Lucifer kept good on her word.

"Here," he motioned. "Why don't you come in?"

Her lips pursed together. "I'm not here for pleasantries. Just give me the contract."

"Marianne, you don't even know what the deal is."

"I don't have to."

"No, you really do."

"Why? What do *you* have to gain from my knowing?"

"My good conscience, that's what!" But just as the words left his mouth he knew how ignorant they sounded.

"Your conscience?" she scoffed. "You watched an innocent woman get tortured and killed, and never said a word to anyone. You don't have a conscience!"

Those words stung, but deep down, he knew she was right.

". . . Never-the-less, I would feel more comfortable if you at least knew the measures of it."

She rolled her eyes. "Fine, tell me."

"Look, are you sure you don't want to come inside . . ?"

"I'm sure. Just tell me."

He sighed. "Well, it requires a lot of sacrifice from you . . ."

"That's okay."

"Just listen to me, please. It's similar to the deal I made. You will get all of the desires of your heart. That is a guarantee. But the price is yourself. You must sign yourself over to Lucifer. You are to give a lifetime of servitude, meanwhile sharing your body with a demon in order to accomplish your tasks. You will not be your own person ever again."

Silence. She gazed soundlessly at the floor, her body beginning to tremble.

"Lucifer," she whispered. "You mean . . ?"

"The devil. Yes. The deal that I was trying to make with you is a deal with the devil."

For a moment, she seemed at loss for words. But then, her voice came out in a whisper. ". . . Wow. You really are evil."

Her words cut right through him.

". . . Yes. And you will be too, if you do this."

She was completely shaken, her hands shaking, her eyes darting in all directions. He longed to hold her in his arms, to comfort her.

She supported her body on the door frame and sighed. ". . . I will do it."

He frowned. "If I may ask, Marianne, why now? Last week, you made it clear you never wanted to see me again."

He expected her to get angry, but she didn't. Instead, her eyes flickered slowly up to his, tears beginning to form.

"It's my mom. The day she got released from the hospital, she relapsed. The cancer spread so quickly, she didn't even have time to call a doctor before she went into a coma. She could die any minute now, and people keep telling me that it's too late. They say I should pull the plug. What do you think, Logan?"

It was his turn to be silent.

What could he possibly say? Yes, pull the plug and save your soul? If he said that, Lucifer would see to both of their deaths. But how could he tell her to sign? That would mean signing away her life, her freedom . . . he was no fool. Lucifer had said that she would get her to sign. He knew, though it put a sour feeling in his stomach. Lucifer put her mother in a coma.

What are you doing, you fool?! The demon said. *She's on the hook.*

I can't ask this of her.

You and I both know that if she doesn't sign, our Master will kill her and you. Is that the depth of your love? Letting her die?

Of course not. But her life . . .

Will go on.

"Logan?" she said, her eyebrows raised. "I asked you what you thought."

He ran a hand through his tussled hair. "I . . . I think you should save her."

She nodded. "I thought so."

"Do . . . are you sure you don't want to come in?"

"No. I just want to get this over with."

Not peeling his gaze from hers, he flicked his hand toward the ground. A sheet of paper appeared in his right hand, the parchment yellowing at the edges. Her eyes widened. In his left hand formed a long, black feather quill with a sharp pointed end like a needle. Her breathing quickened, as if this suddenly made it all real.

"Where's the ink?" she asked quietly.

"You are the ink."

She grimaced as she held out her palm. He brought up the pen and jabbed her finger. She flinched. Blood trickled forth. He dipped the quill gently in the blood and held the pen out to her. She took it with a shaking hand, tears streaming down her face.

"Were . . . were you happy?" she asked as she stared at the black pen, dripping with her blood. "After making the deal, were you happy?"

He had to think about this. The truth was, after the demon's presence was established, he hadn't felt much of anything. It wasn't until Marianne that his human emotions started to resurface.

". . . I wasn't unhappy."

This answer seemed to satisfy her. She put the pen to the paper, signing a sloppy red signature. The words shined for a moment before the paper and quill started to disintegrate, the edges burning until the items vanished into thin air. No doubt they were being delivered to Lucifer.

She stood stiffly in the doorway. "It's done?"

"It's done."

"So now my mother will be healed?"

"Yes."

She let out a deep breath. It sounded as if she'd been holding it all night. "Good. I don't feel any different, though."

"You won't at first. The demon will come into you slowly. It will probably be a few days before the process is complete."

She nodded to indicate she understood. "Logan, can I ask you something?"

"Anything."

"Not that I plan on breaking it, but is there a way out of the deal? Just in case?"

"Yes. But I doubt you will try it."

"Why not?"

"Because you most likely already have. There is only one being that can break a deal with Lucifer, and that is Lucifer's enemy."

" . . . Got it."

She looked away from him, turning her back towards the door. "Good bye, then."

She stalked off, leaving him staring soundlessly after her.

Chapter 13

Logan paced around the hotel room.

The carpet sunk beneath his toes, his mind in a hazy whirl. He was still thinking about last night. Marianne signed the contract, which meant that their lives were saved. But what did it mean beyond that? What did it mean for him? For her?

He could feel the demon's aggravation at his racing thoughts, but he didn't care. He had to figure things out.

The problem was, he didn't know what influence the demon would have on Marianne. He longed for her to stay exactly the same. Perhaps it was wishful thinking . . . not that it mattered. Her aloofness from the night before affirmed what he already knew. She never wanted to see him again.

But maybe not. Her human emotions would likely be subdued once the demon took over. Could that include her grief over Emily's murder? Without grief, maybe she could forget. Without grief, maybe she would be willing to give him a second chance.

Then they could finally be together.

His heart expanded in his chest as he ran to the bathroom, fixing his hair and throwing on a pair of shoes. He didn't care if she threw him out. He had to see her.

~~

He arrived at her doorstep twenty minutes later. The blank sheet of wood loomed over him, its dull handle shining faintly in the light. He suddenly didn't want to knock. The entrance to her apartment no longer seemed an entrance to his salvation, but to his doom. He wondered what spurred this feeling.

He took a deep breath and forced his knuckles against the wood, sounding out three loud knocks. He waited on the doorstep for a whole minute, his foot tapping on the floor.

No answer.

He gave three more knocks.

Another minute. No answer.

He sighed with frustration and placed his hand on the knob. To his surprise, it was unlocked.

"Marianne?"

No reply. He opened the door. The door traveled inward and revealed Marianne, who was sitting by the window, her hair in disarray, her face blank.

"Marianne?"

She continued to stare silently. He approached her, sitting beside her on the white leather couch. "Mari, it's me. Logan."

She didn't even look at him. It was as if he wasn't there.

"... Do you want to talk about anything?"

Silence.

His eyes flickered to the silver cellphone that sat beside her. It beamed with missed calls and messages from her mother.

"Hey, your mom has been calling! That must mean she's healed, right? Isn't that great?"

She still said nothing. He leaned back, dumbfounded. She hadn't even answered her mother's calls. It was so unlike her. He placed his hands awkwardly in his lap.

"Okay, that's fine. We don't have to talk. We'll just sit here, okay? We'll sit here and stare."

Her glazed eyes gave no sign of encouragement. He stayed seated beside her, staring with her out of the small, glass window.

~~~

He had sat at that window for two hours with her. She never moved an inch.

This irked him more than he liked. He wasn't sure the reason for her silence, but one thing was for sure.

She was changing.

He decided he would visit her the next day. Hopefully the demon would be fully infested within three days; that was the standard time for a change. He thought back to his own transformation. The first day, his thoughts had begun to darken, and his heart felt as if it were being coated with ice. On the second day his thoughts were even more sinister, and he could feel another presence within him. Then, on the third day, the demon's voice echoed for the first time in his head, sending cold, unfamiliar chills along his spine. Within the first year, their thoughts conjoined into one mind. He soon couldn't imagine life without his other half.

Now he wanted nothing more than to be rid of it.

He never did stare blankly in silence, though. So why was Marianne? He supposed different demons must have various effects on people. Or perhaps she was simply grieving. After all, her involvement in the deal had not been completely voluntary like Logan's was.

Maybe he would find out the next day.

~~~

Logan once again treaded the stairs that led to her apartment. His leather jacket was dusted with droplets from the long mist that had stretched across the air, forcing everyone outside into a wave of floating water. He bounded up the last steps and stood at that familiar blank door. He knocked three times.

No answer.

He turned the rusty knob and found that the door was unlocked. He pushed it, letting it swing open with a slow creak.

"Marianne?"

He peered inside. She was there, sitting in the same spot near the window. Her hair looked more tangled than before, and her shirt from the day before seemed to sag on her thin body. She must have been sitting there all night.

He shut the door behind him as he walked further inside. He trailed into the living room, peering at the side of her face.

". . . Marianne?"

This time, her head swung around, her dark eyes staring like two glassy orbs into his face. They were dull, no light reflecting off them.

He took another step towards her. ". . . Are you there?"

A cruel smile began to form. The smile widened and turned into laughter; cold, uncontrollable laughter that echoed throughout the room and filled up the expanse of space.

Logan froze. He wanted to run, but the demon wanted to stay and observe the progress of its client. He felt as if he were being pulled in every direction.

He waited for that maniacal laughter to finally die before he took a seat on the couch. She turned her gaze from him and back to the window, her battered reflection against the misting glass. She continued to ignore him, sounding out random spurts of laughter as time progressed.

Though this version of Marianne disturbed him, he knew he could not leave. He would be there for her until the change was complete. He was set on that.

They watched as the sun finally began to sink in the sky, sending out a purple-orange light that reminded Logan of their time in Central Park. How things had changed since then.

Finally, as stars began to scatter along the night sky, he fell back on the leather, allowing his eyes to rest until he slipped into a deep sleep.

~~~

He didn't remember where he was at first. But as he looked at the oak coffee table and grasped the leather, he knew. He turned to the window, where gray light from a hood of foreboding rain clouds shown through. The chair in front of it was empty.

Marianne was gone.

"Marianne?!"

Logan shot up. She was not in the kitchen. He rushed to her bedroom. The bed was empty and unmade. He jogged to her bathroom, knocking on the door furiously. But as he touched the knob, he found that it was unlocked, and peered inside. Empty.

She had left the apartment.

He ran through the front door and bounded down the steps, thunder booming behind him. Her empty laughter still echoed in his mind.

He broke through the glass doors of the complex and stared out at the street, the mist clinging to his skin. He was about to track down a cab, when he heard something. He stopped. He could hear that familiar chuckle carrying lightly into the air. He turned around, going down the sidewalk and towards the source of the voice. He approached the side of the building where a narrow alleyway stood.

He could see Marianne's back, her long hair damp. He jogged into the dark alley. When he was just a few feet away from her, she spoke for the first time:

"Three days. A spot on prediction, Logan."

He fought a shiver that threatened to pass through him. "What are you doing out here?"

She turned around, and he stumbled back. She was drenched in blood. A knife was positioned in her left hand, the body of a dead tabby cat in the other. She let the cat's body fall to the ground, its eyes still wide with fear.

"I saw it out the window," she cooed. "It just looked so cute and lonely. I thought I'd come down and give it some company."

Her expression was that of mock innocence. It made him sick.

"Marianne . . ." he breathed.

"Well don't look so surprised, Logan. You are the one who did this. You made me!"

"I . . . I didn't think . . ."

"Oh come on! You put a demon inside me. What did you think would happen?"

When he was silent, she smiled devilishly.

"Dear, dear Logan. Did you really think that I would not be tampered with? That I would realize my love for you, and run like a lost lamb into your arms?"

He took a shaky breath. ". . . I just hoped you might forgive me."

"Forgiveness is a tool of the weak," she sneered. "A cop out for those afraid of confrontation. Real power lies with anger. With vengeance." She cocked her head to the side. "And to think that the

Great Liar, an ancient demon of immense power, is trapped beneath the soul of a weak, little human. Such a pity."

He could feel the demon rising furiously within him. He did his best to push it down, and his insides burned like fire.

". . . You said, vengeance?" he asked through clenched teeth.

She chuckled. "Don't worry. As much as I'd like to, I won't seek revenge on you. As long as you are a servant of the Master, I can't touch you."

"This demon has taught you a lot, then?"

"More than any being on this Earth. And to think I once believed in love and kindness! As if those could grant me my desires. What lies are told among the human race in order to keep them from killing one another. Perhaps your demon does not deserve his title, Logan. Perhaps it is mankind that is the Great Liar."

Not one word sounded like Marianne. It was like her body was a shell for evil.

He started to wonder if *he* knew the true terms of the deal.

". . . And what are your desires, Marianne?"

A small giggle escaped from her lips. "Death, of course."

She took the bloody knife and placed it in her pocket. "You were right about one thing, Logan. Nature holds no significance. It is what people do that is magnificent.

I'll see you around."

With that she turned around, her hips swaying back and forth until her body vanished like a wisp into the air.

Chapter 14

Logan wandered down the glistening street. It had started to rain, and the droplets came down like stones on his body. The darkened sky sent gray rays along the stone buildings, the whole street sparkling with mist. He trudged through the rippling puddles as he peered with at the ground, his mind in a whirl.

Would you calm down? The Great Liar said. *You got what you wanted.*

"This isn't what I wanted," he said out loud.

So you didn't get the girl. So what? She is more powerful than either of us could have imagined. Not only have you saved her life, you've given her the greatest of gifts.

"A gift . . ." Laughter escaped from him.

"Logan?"

A woman's voice. He whipped around. Satan stood before him, a bright red dress hugging her body, her dark winged makeup untouched by the pouring rain. She walked up to him, her heels clicking against the concrete. She smiled.

"Logan, my boy. You did it. You got her to sign the contract; with my help, of course."

"You put her mother in a coma."

She shrugged. "It wasn't hard. The old woman was practically on her death bed. I just sped up the process."

He was silent, and she gazed at him with a vague curiosity.

"Smile, Logan. You did it. You have pleased your master."

"Sorry . . . I just don't feel like smiling right now."

"Because you didn't get to be with your little bunny?" she jeered, her lip protruded. Suddenly, her eyes narrowed, and her exaggerated expression turned into a frown. "You knew you could never be together. You signed a contract, binding yourself solely to me. You are *mine*. And now, so is she."

"That wasn't her." He took a shaky step forward. "I just spoke with her, and that was not her. That was full on possession."

She chuckled. "Do you honestly think that? She is no less possessed than you were."

"No, the demon and I were equal . . ."

"The deal is the same!" He flinched at the outburst. "She is just as influenced as you once were, and are *going* to be."

She began advancing towards him. He stumbled back, but not before she clasped onto his cheeks, digging her razor nails into his skin. His breathing quickened as she brought his face to hers.

"You listen to me, Logan Lokte." Her eyes blazed. "I will not have to step in again. Your little rebellion will end. You will go back into your hole, and let my demon take back what is legally his. You *will* do your job next time. If you don't, I will personally terminate the project by reaching into your chest and taking out your still beating heart. My demon will be assigned to a new body, and your soul will be

(107)

left to rot for eternity in your own, personalized pit. Am I understood?"

He gasped for air as she lifted his feet off the ground. He could feel the warm blood trickling slowly down his neck.

"AM I UNDERSTOOD?!" Her voice transformed into a menacing dual tone.

"Yes! I understand, I understand . . ."

"Good."

She released him, and he fell onto the wet pavement, the water sending shivers through his body. She gazed at him for a moment before kneeling beside him, her right hand tracing his bloody cheek. She offered a smile that did not reflect the emptiness in her eyes.

"Do not fear, my boy. This was simply a mishap, a small glitch in a much larger system. Once you start adhering to the contract again, all will be set right, and you will go back to being one of my favorite servants. Just do as you're told, and you will be rewarded."

She sounded so soothing. He almost couldn't believe she threatened him with agonizing death seconds ago.

She patted him lightly on the leg and stood up. She started to turn away. As much as he didn't want to, Logan had to ask her something.

"Wait!"

She looked back.

"Vengeance. Marianne is the demon of vengeance, isn't she?"

"Vengeance and destruction," she replied, amused. "She's a masterpiece, Logan. She has been waiting for a viable body for centuries. And now, she is finally released."

"What purpose do you have for her?"

"Vengeance and destruction of course. To hunt down all those that once wronged her. And then, when she is done, she will begin her real killing, and the apocalypse can begin."

He stopped. "The . . . the apocalypse?"

"Have you not noticed our increased activity this past century? Yes. All these years of petty battles for souls has led up to this moment. The destruction she will bring upon this Earth is my first large scale attack on His people. Then, the real war will begin."

She looked down suddenly, as if something had caught her attention. "Well, my boy, I'm afraid I must leave you. Do clean yourself up. I'm sure we will see each other quite soon."

Her body flickered for a moment before she vanished, leaving him alone on the shining street.

He hoisted himself up and wiped his bleeding face. The rain was pouring harder now. A loud strike of thunder filled the sky. His head throbbed. Marianne, a tool for murder and destruction . . . the apocalypse . . . it was all his fault. Logan Lokte, an average guy from the city, had become a player in the beginning of the apocalypse.

He dragged his feet along the ground, a hand held to his head. Guilt . . . such an unfamiliar feeling, yet it plagued every inch of him. What was he doing? Why had he agreed to let Marianne become Satan's puppet? If he loved her like he thought he did, he surely would have put a stop to it. Perhaps death would have been better.

He looked up at the murky clouds, where another flash of lightning lit up the sky. He thought of Jasmine. That sweet smile, beautiful green eyes. She always had a way of seeing the good in people. What did she think of him now? Could she see any good in his blackened heart?

His knees felt like jelly. He clutched onto a lamp post.

The demon whispered lowly in his ear. *Logan, that life is past. She is gone. You must move on.*

How? He answered. *She is the whole reason I agreed to work for Lucifer in the first place. How do you expect me to move on?*

Well then continue what you started. Avenge her. Avenge her and your unborn child, just as you once vowed.

I did. I killed the driver.

Ah, but he is not the only one to blame, is he? We both know who is at fault here. He took her, He is the one who allowed her to die. He could have stopped it, yet He didn't. Take vengeance. Take vengeance on Him and all those who work for Him.

He considered this for a moment.

Of course, we both know what has to happen, the demon continued. *You heard our Master. If you just let me back in . . .*

"No!"

Logan, she has commanded . . .

"NO!" He hoisted himself higher onto the lamppost. "You have controlled me for too long. And to think I actually believed we were working together . . . but not anymore."

You can't get rid of me, it seethed. *I am a part of your contract. You are bound to me!*

"All this time, I thought you could help me. I thought you could help me learn to live again. But I was wrong. You have taken everything! And now, Marianne . . . you took an innocent woman, someone that I loved . . ."

It was a job!

Logan's face was flushing. "No. No, what it was, was evil. Blatantly hurting the innocent for your own cruel pleasure. Well I'm not going to be part of it anymore."

. . . What are you saying, Logan?

He looked up at the thundering sky, the rain pouring onto his face. How had he not seen it before? Four years, he had been shrouded in darkness. But he had been shown the light. Marianne had showed him the light. Now he knew why he had met her. Why he had glimpsed her in the first place, why he could not tear himself away from her. She had been brought to him, presented to him by a higher power . . . so that he could be saved.

"God," he breathed. "Forgive me."

A piercing noise rang throughout his body. He doubled over as the demon screamed, his chest radiating in painful convulsions. He squinted through the droplets and down the winding street. Ahead, he could see a metal cross, suspended on the top of a towering cathedral. He let go of the slick lamppost and barreled that way, his feet shaking beneath him. The demon continued to scream, the sound rising until it and the cathedral were all he could focus on. If only he could reach it. All his limbs were beginning to burn with the noise; his vision was blurring. He kept running. He was getting closer . . .

The scream turned into a deafening roar as he reached the two large doors, the Gothic stone dripping with water. He pushed on the doors and fell onto a floor.

The scream died instantly. The Great Liar trembled within. He began moving down the aisle, gazing up at the golden cross that stood high on the platform.

He built up every ounce of courage within him.

"My Father, who art in Heaven. Hallowed be thy name . . ."

The demon retaliated by sending intense rays of pain in his chest and stomach. He cried out and leaned against one of the pews, clutching onto his burning chest.

Logan, it pleaded. *Stop.*

". . . Thy kingdom come, they will be done, on Earth as it is in Heaven."

Another shot of pain. He stumbled, nearly falling onto the floor.

"Give us each day our daily bread, and forgive us of our sins, as we forgive those who sin against us . . ."

His chest was on fire. He screamed and toppled onto the marble. Blood dropped from the torn skin on his elbow. He was so close to the platform now. He looked up at the golden cross, which displayed a metal Jesus, its eyes seeming to stare right at him.

Logan, you don't have to do this. You can have control. You can have anything you want. Just don't . . .

"And lead us not into temptation," he growled. "But deliver us . . ."

Another scream. He was on fire now. He thought he might die, right there and then . . .

"Deliver us . . ."

LOGAN, NO!

"FROM EVIL!"

A clash of thunder crackled across the sky. The double doors of the cathedral flew open, and misty wind whooshed into the room. He cried out as the wind circled around him. He could feel it. The Great Liar was being frayed, torn from his fragile body. It felt like he was being ripped apart. Soon he could not even hear his own screams over the gusting wind.

Then, it stopped. The wind ceased instantaneously, and all the pain diminished. The inside of the cathedral stood still, its doors swinging gently from the stormy wind.

He stood up. Everything felt different. He was tired, weaker than he had been before. But his mind felt free.

He walked down the long marble aisle. He felt lighter, like every weight that had been placed upon him was lifted.

He broke into the cool night air, where the rain was still flowing to the ground. He gazed up at the flashing clouds. He could see it again. He could see the wonder of the moving sky, the majesty of the roaring thunder. The rain renewed him, like a million drops of God's forgiveness pouring down. All was peace. He could feel the Holy Spirit coursing through him; feelings of love, and of hope. And as he peered at that endless gray sky shining with light, he could feel God's power in everything around him.

He let out a cry of redemption that echoed into the air and traveled upward, as if absorbed into the sky and reaching up into the Heavens. He was a new man. Reborn.

But as his cry reached its last note, he began to get weary. He reached out to grab onto something, but there was nothing around him. His body toppled unwillingly onto the concrete. He stared at the sky for one last second before his eyes closed, the world slowly fading into blackness.

Part II: The Rise

Chapter 15

Logan awoke to the sound of dripping water.

Long wooden beams on an arched ceiling. Orange light flooding the room through large, angled windows. Where had he seen this place before?

As his eyes trailed to the golden cross at the end of the aisle, he remembered.

He jolted up, only for his head to throb suddenly. Pain . . . but no voice. No constant internal monitor. He had forgotten what it was like to be the master of his own mind. It was refreshing, like a ray of sun breaking through a murky cloud. He smiled at the cross that beamed back at him, light reflecting off its shiny surface.

"Thank you."

"LOGAN!" A voice interrupted.

He turned to the sound. At first, the man running toward him appeared like a blurry blob. But as he got closer, Logan began to recognize the features; short black, curly hair, dark skin, a short but burly build, and big brown eyes. Loose, tattered clothing flapped behind him.

He observed every familiar feature, but could not believe his eyes. He was like a ghost from Logan's past. He represented the time when he had a normal, human life . . . something didn't think he would never get back.

The guy knelt over him, sticking his face uncomfortably close to his.

"Logan! Logan, you alright?"

". . . Tom?" he muttered.

"Yeah man, it's me. You want me to help you up?"

He nodded. Tom held out a strong arm, which he reached for thankfully, pulling his abdomen off the wooden ground. He peered in awe at his old friend. Thomas Jackson, his college roommate and lifelong comrade. Though Tom only stayed at college for a year, he and Logan had remained best friends. Besides Jasmine, he'd never been closer to anyone. But he had not seen Tom in over four years.

"I saw you laying outside, so I carried you in," Tom explained. "I couldn't believe it was you."

"I know." Logan's voice was scratchy. "It's been a long time."

"Yeah, it has."

There was an awkward silence.

". . . So how did you find me? Have you gone to this church before?" Logan asked.

"Yeah. This is where I go now on Sundays."

"Oh. It's beautiful."

"Yup. They're good people."

Another silence.

"Okay man, you want to tell me why you were lying outside in a puddle? You're not homeless, are you?"

Logan smiled. "No."

"Good. Because you know after four years, I'm not sharing my bed!"

He laughed. "Well, you don't have to worry about that. I have a suite downtown."

"A suite downtown? What're you doing here?"

A good question. How was he supposed to explain these past four years? Tom would think he was insane.

". . . I was walking, and I fell down."

Tom raised his eyebrows. "Way to be cryptic, dude."

"Well, I can't . . ."

Before he could finish, his gaze shifted to the two wooden doors, the crack in between them sending a ray of light in the room. He pushed himself to his feet.

"Logan, where you going?"

He dragged his feet toward the double doors. Sunlight; a beauty he had not been able to appreciate in four years. His shoes clicked against the wood as he walked forward, placing his hand firmly on the brass handle. He swung the door open.

Sunlight bathed him, enveloping him in a big, warm embrace. The air was still thick with precipitation, a bright blue sky was forming behind white, fluffy clouds. It was all so beautiful. But what was most amazing was the tiny rainbow that extended along the sky. Red, green, blue, yellow; the colors shined through the misty air, like a ray of hope stretched along the Heavens. He smiled. The gray man-made buildings were nothing in comparison. This, with its color and majesty . . . this was real beauty.

"Logan, what the hell are you doing?"

He turned to see a dumbfounded Tom staring at him.

"Oh. I . . ."

A chilling memory suddenly invaded him.

Marianne.

Marianne was in the clutches of a powerful demon, a demon that threatened to bring on the apocalypse and end humanity. What was he doing standing here? He had to stop her before it was too late.

"I've got to go."

"What?"

Logan ran forward and raised his arm in the air. "Taxi!"

One of the yellow cars halted in front of him. He nearly leapt into the seat. But before he could shut the door, Tom hopped in, forcing Logan over and shutting the door behind him.

"What are you doing?"

"I could ask you the same question!" he fumed.

"I'm going somewhere that you can't go."

"Like hell. You were my best friend, Logan. We run into each other after four years, and after two minutes of talking, you try to drive off? No, I want to know what happened to you, and I'm not leaving until you tell me."

Guilt panged his chest. "I'm sorry. I'll explain later, but what I have to do right now is really dangerous. You can't come."

"Dangerous? Did you get in with the wrong people?"

". . . Something like that."

The driver whipped around, glaring at the passengers with narrow eyes. "I need to know where I'm going, guys."

Logan held a hand towards the driver. "Okay, just give us a minute! Tom, this is really dangerous. Like, scary dangerous. You can't come. I'm not risking your life."

Tom reached behind him, grabbing the strap of his seat belt and clicking it beside him.

"It's not your life to risk. I'm going."

Logan sighed. The driver was still peering at them, greasy black hair swept to the side of his face. "Well? Where to?"

For a second, Logan was at loss of what to do. But seeing as Tom was not changing his mind, he put a hand to his face and muttered the address.

The taxi sped forward.

"So since it's out there, you mind telling me where you've been these past four years?"

". . . It's complicated."

"Complicated?" Tom scoffed. "No man, what's complicated is when your best friend just vanishes. Doesn't tell anyone where he's going, or when he'll be back. Some people assume he is dead. Then all of sudden, years later, you find that friend lying unconscious in front of your church. 'It's complicated' isn't going to cut it. You're going to have to tell me what happened."

"You wouldn't believe me if I told you."

"Try me."

He growled in frustration. Why couldn't he just leave it alone?

"Alright, I'll tell you."

Tom perked up, his eyes wide.

". . . I sold my soul to the devil."

He leaned back in his seat and placed his arms over his chest. "That's so not funny, dude."

"I told you that you wouldn't believe me," he muttered. Tom looked in his direction for a moment, then turned towards the window. They were quiet for several minutes, the wheels of the car rolling gently beneath them. Logan's mind raced.

He didn't have a plan. What was he going to say to Marianne? How could he possibly stop her from the chaos she was about to bring? It was unthinkable, knowing that *she* was the one who was to start the apocalypse. Now, with Tom tagging along, everything was just more complicated. He closed his eyes and said a silent prayer.

Lord, please forgive me for what I've done. Help me to stop it. Help me to fix the problems I have caused . . . to save Marianne. Please, God. Help me save her.

He sighed, allowing his eyes to wander among the gray buildings and sleek cars that flashed past the window. He trusted that God would help him, but in the end, it all depended on Marianne. He hoped she would make the right decision. After all, if he, of all people could be saved, so could she.

The taxi soon came to a rolling stop in front of Marianne's apartment. Logan jumped out. Tom followed, tripping over the curb and stumbling back onto his feet. Logan gazed at him sullenly.

"This is your last chance, Tom. If you come with me, there's no turning back. I don't know what we'll find."

"Well since you still haven't told me what happened, I guess I'll just have to come up with you to . . . wherever it is we're going."

"I already told you! Ugh . . ." He slapped his hand against his head. "Fine. Just stay behind me. I don't know if she's still here."

"She? You're in trouble with a she?"

He didn't respond. He marched through the glass door, stomping up the wooden stairs. They creaked dangerously beneath his feet. Three flights later, he was standing once again on Marianne's doorstep. This time, the door was shut. He wiggled the resisting knob.

Tom snorted. "A locked door. Real dangerous, dude."

Logan frowned. He raised his fist, ready to bang hard on the blank door; but just as he was about to do this, a long creaking sound rang out. The previously locked door opened as if by itself.

Tom's eyes went wide. He followed Logan into the foreboding silence. The apartment was dark. The only light came from the outside window, which was darkened by a gray curtain. It appeared deserted, but Logan could feel something. A presence, like they were being watched.

He searched the space.

"Marianne? Are you there, Marianne?"

Silence. He stepped into the living room. Something stained the white couch. He knelt beside it and peered closely. On the top of the cushion, a dark red droplet formed a perfect semi-circle.

Blood.

The blood was situated into a trail of tiny drops, extending toward the bedroom, which was cut off by a set of light blue curtains. At first, he feared it might be Marianne's blood. But considering she was a demon now, that wasn't likely.

Tom wrung his hands together. "Logan, is that what I think it is . . ?"

"Yes."

"I think we should get out of here . . ."

Logan began to follow the blood trail. Tom sighed, but stayed close behind. They approached the blue floral curtain, which was stained with a puddle of blood that extended along the bottom of the fabric. Logan grabbed the curtain tentatively. It was coarse between his fingers. Taking a deep breath, he yanked it open.

They both jumped back.

On the ceiling, hanging from an entanglement of barbwire, was Christopher Ballard. His body was sprawled out, his legs torn apart and his arms hanging like wings to the side. The barbwire cut tiny holes into his flesh that dripped with red blood. His torn shirt showcased a large, bloody wound in his stomach that flooded onto the bed below, and around his open body hung strings of bright yellow lights that lit up the room. Above his still open eyes, there was a bloody star carved deep into his forehead.

"He always called me his bright star."

They whipped around. Marianne was standing behind them, her posture casual, expression blank. Her hair was down, forming perfectly ringlets down her back. She wore a corset top and skinny jeans, her eyes appearing like sharp, black wings.

Logan's insides knotted with fear.

"He said that I would shine, like a star in the lights of Broadway. Well he was wrong. And now he's my star." Her dark eyes traced Logan's body. "You seem different."

". . . You do, too."

"Yes, well I have been blessed with a new life. But you seem weaker than before." She gazed at his companion. "And who is this?"

He could barely get the sound out of his throat: "I'm T-Tom."

She appeared amused. "Doubting Thomas, indeed. Tell me Tom, is this the first dead body you have seen?"

"Y-Yes."

"Well, don't worry," she said with an evil grin. "There will be plenty more to come."

"Marianne, you have to stop this!" Logan said.

Her eyes narrowed. "What?"

"You . . . you can't keep doing this. For your own sake. You're being used. Lucifer never cared about you, she is just using you to start the final battle so that you can bring on the apocalypse! I didn't know that was her purpose until after you had signed the deal. Please believe me."

To his surprise, she began to laugh.

"Oh, Logan! You honestly thought I did not know that? I know my purpose. The demon has told me."

He was dumbstruck. "But the only reason you signed the contract was to become a successful actress and to cure your mother! Do you not care about those things anymore?"

"No." She shrugged. "I don't."

She began advancing towards him. He tried to stand his ground.

"Those were the petty cries of a weak human, surrounded by other fragile, crying humans. Miniscule specks in a much larger world.

I will get revenge on those who have wronged me. But after that, I will become a player in a real game: the onslaught of the apocalypse."

"But . . . why? How does that benefit you?"

"The honor of sitting at the Master's right hand, of course. Plus, I get to help end the cries of the pathetic humans."

Tom began to mutter a prayer under his breath: "Though I walk through the valley of the shadow of death, I shall fear no evil, for Thou art with . . ."

Marianne struck his cheek, forcing his body down onto the hardwood floor. His face was streaked with blood.

"There is no God here!"

"Yes there is!" Logan rushed forward and offered a hand to Tom. "And He still loves you."

She looked taken aback as Logan dusted off Tom's clothes. Her gaze then sharpened, nostrils flaring wildly.

"I knew you were different," she seethed. "You have turned to *Him*."

"Yes."

"TRAITOR!"

They stumbled backwards. She marched towards them, her body hot and rigid. She backed them up towards the open front door, until they stood directly on the edge of the staircase. Logan gazed at her in terror. Her lips parted slightly.

"You have betrayed me, and our Master. Your protection is now void."

She flung her hand upward. An invisible force pushed on both their chests, and they began to fly down the staircase.

Chapter 16

They struck the steps, their bodies turning round and round into the sharp wooden corners. It seemed like an eternity before they finally stopped, each landing on the other. Logan lifted a bruised leg out from under Tom and crawled into a sitting position. He could feel warm blood pouring from his forehead.

Tom lifted his upper body off the floor, his abdomen still touching the hardwood. He was bleeding as well, with fresh scrapes covering his arms and a bloody gash notched into his lower lip. They were silent for a moment, attempting to regain their strength.

"How . . . how do we have no serious injuries?" Logan held a hand to his wound. "That could've killed us."

"I think God is watching over us, buddy. We should go, in . . . in case she follows us."

Logan tried to lift his leg, which shot with pain. "Good idea, let's go . . ."

Logan's leg gave out. He nearly toppled to the floor, but Tom caught him, offering his shoulder for support. He leaned his left side on him as they wobbled out the glass doors. A chaotic city greeted them. Large buildings, cars that flew by on the street. They hailed down a cab and stumbled into the back.

"Woah!" the driver said, peering back at them with wide eyes. "What happened to you guys? You need me to take you to a hospital or something?"

Tom answered first. "Yeah, maybe we should . . ."

"No!" Logan interjected. "No, we need to go to my suite downtown."

He gave the address, after which the driver sped out into a sea of traffic.

"What's in your hotel downtown?" Tom clicked his seatbelt with a shaking hand.

"I have supplies there. Medical supplies that we can use. And besides. I think we need somewhere private to talk."

"Yeah, we really do."

They were quiet for the rest of the way as their minds raced. Logan could still see Christopher Ballard, his desecrated body strung up like a mutilated star. Dead people did not phase him when he was half-demon, but now Ballard's image kept surfacing in his vision, making his insides twist violently. And Marianne . . . in only a few short days, it seemed like every trace of her was gone. He wondered if there was any part of her left to save.

He thought back to the past four years, living with a demon inside him. It still felt strange to be free from that. He remembered just weeks ago, looking at Emily's mutilated body and feeling nothing but contempt towards Sallos for bending the rules. All that time striking deals, signing contracts. All those innocent people he tricked into working for the devil. Where were they now? Wasting their eternal souls, no doubt. Just like he would have been had he not met

Marianne. How could everything change so much in a day? How could he have been so selfish? Because of him all of those people, including a woman he loved, were on the path to damnation.

He closed his eyes, silent tears treading down his cheeks, his forehead set against the window. He hadn't had time to grieve over what he had done, and it was all hitting him at once. It was overwhelming.

Minutes later they arrived at his hotel, a sleek white building that towered into the sky. He wiped the tears from his eyes. He handed a wad of money to the driver and the two of them wobbled out, Logan sporting a limp.

They entered through a set of automatic doors and went into the lobby, which was adorned with plush carpet and tropical palm trees that lined the sitting area. He led Tom to the elevators. But just as they were about to get in, he felt his back pocket for his room key. It was empty. He sighed and searched the insides of his wallet, then checked his other pockets. Nothing.

"It must have fallen out during our spill on the stairs," he told Tom.

They traveled back to the front desk, where a guest representative sat. She greeted them with a smile.

"How may I help you gentlemen?"

"I think I lost my room key," Logan said. "I was wondering if I could get another one."

"Of course. What is your room number?"

"1003."

She typed rapidly into her computer. Her eyes searched the screen.

"1003 . . . for Logan Lokte?"

"Yes, ma'am."

Her eyes narrowed, her lip jutted in confusion. "I'm sorry sir, but it says here that you checked out earlier today."

"What? No, I never checked out. Did you put in the right room number?"

"1003 for Logan Lokte, yes. Was there anyone staying in the room with you? Maybe . . ."

"No, no there was nobody. Look, I've been staying here for weeks. All my stuff is up there. If it says I'm checked out, where is all my stuff?"

For a moment, she seemed at loss of what to do.

"Umm, hold on sir. Let me have housekeeping go up and check . . ."

She raised the phone to her ear and dialed a number. Logan leaned wearily on the marble stand, a hand pressed to his forehead. Dried blood rubbed off on his fingers.

"Well is this crazy, or what?" Tom mumbled.

Logan didn't respond. Stress pounded in his temple. He wanted to yell, to punch a wall in anger, or even just break down and cry.

After several long minutes, she received a call back. Her eyes widened, and Logan knew the response was not good. She placed the phone back on the receiver.

". . . Sir, housekeeping said that there was nothing left in the room. They already cleaned it and everything. It's empty."

He felt like he'd been struck in the gut. He leaned his forehead on the cold marble.

"Mr. Lokte, are you sure that no one else had access to your room or your account?"

"No . . ." he began to reply. His mind flashed to when he first purchased the room. Lucifer ensured that he would have a place to live, as well as sufficient funds to sustain himself. He reached into his wallet and grabbed the red credit card that she had given him, staring at it blankly.

"Sir?" the representative interrupted his thoughts.

"Would you tell me if this card is working?" he asked, almost absently.

". . . I'm afraid I would need you to make a purchase to know, sir."

"That's okay. Try to purchase me another room."

She did not object. She took the card and began typing in her computer.

"Would you like smoking or non-smoking?"

"Either."

She typed a few more words, then attempted to swipe the card. The computer made a loud beeping noise. She blinked and tried to swipe again. Another beeping noise. She handed it back to him.

". . . I'm afraid it's declined."

He stared at the card for a moment, and began to laugh. The gravity of his situation bore on him like bricks, and instead of crying or yelling, he erupted into hysterical laughter.

Both Tom and the representative gazed with alarm.

". . . It's okay dude, we'll find somewhere else to go. Thank you, ma'am."

She nodded. Tom grabbed his old friend by the shoulder, hoisting him from the lobby and back out to the double glass doors. They stood awkwardly outside while cars zoomed by on the street. Logan was still smiling, spastic chuckles arising from his lips.

"Okay, we've obviously had a really bad day," Tom said. "But right now, we need to figure out where we are going."

"The card was declined." Logan ignored Tom's concerns. "And all my stuff is gone. I guess they know now. The contract really is broken, and everything with it!"

Tom had no idea what he was talking about, nor did he care. He just needed to get him somewhere other than the busy sidewalk.

"Alright, I have an idea. Come on."

Tom hailed a cab, and minutes later, they sat across from each other in a tiny coffee shop. The room was empty apart from themselves and one person behind the counter. The walls were decorated with local art, its floors made of a light, splintering hardwood. Both had a cup of coffee clasped in their hands, staring blankly at one another.

". . . Why here?" Logan finally asked, glancing at the barista wiping the laminate counters. "I thought we needed somewhere private?"

"We couldn't go to my place. I have two roommates who would badger me 'til who knows when if they saw me like this. Besides, it's not like this place is exactly public."

Logan nodded as he sipped on black coffee. It was bitter, but refreshing.

Tom's eyes narrowed. "Now I think you owe me an explanation. That girl . . . that *thing* . . . it wasn't human, was it?"

He grimaced. Hearing Marianne referred to as a "thing" put a sour taste in his mouth.

"No, she is; sort of."

He shook his head. "Man, you've got to tell me more than that."

He sighed and set his cup on the rickety table. "Well, the truth is, she's not much different than I was just yesterday."

"What do you mean?"

He told him. He told his whole story, from the day Jasmine died to signing the contract with Marianne. As much as he wanted to conceal all of his failures, he left no detail out. His dealings, Sallos, his encounters with the devil, the coming of the apocalypse. Tom gazed at him throughout, his eyes wide with intrigue. When he was finally finished, Tom leaned back in his chair, peering thoughtfully out the window.

". . . So you see why I didn't want to involve you in it," Logan said.

"Yeah, I do." He was silent for a moment. ". . . I'm sorry."

"For tagging along? It's okay. I probably wouldn't have stayed sane . . ."

"No, Logan. I'm sorry for what happened to you."

He was taken aback. He said nothing in response.

". . . I'm sorry about Jasmine," Tom continued. "I didn't hear what happened until days after. I went to your place as soon as I found out, but you were already gone. And then you got tricked into a deal with . . . man, I am so sorry. I wish I had gotten to you before all this happened. Maybe I could have done something . . ."

"Hey, don't be sorry. I chose my own path. And anyways, I'm back now, right?"

Tom smirked. "A good thing, too. The world has missed you, buddy."

Logan smiled. "Honestly Tom, I'm surprised you believe me. I figured you'd have run off at this point."

"Well, when she pushed us down the stairs without even touching us, I knew that we weren't dealing with anything normal. Plus, there was all the cryptic apocalypse talk."

"That obvious, huh?"

"Just a little bit."

Logan's smiled faded. "You still can, you know."

"Can what?"

". . . Run off. I'm the one who got us into this mess. You've been through a lot already, there's no need for you to keep tagging along. You just keep yourself out of more danger."

He nodded thoughtfully, as if turning his words over in his head. The sun was setting over the horizon, casting a purple-orange light on his face.

"So you're still going to try to save her?"

"Yes. I have to."

He sighed and shook his head. "I don't think it's a good idea, but if that's the path you choose . . . I'm behind you."

Logan was shocked. "And endanger your own life? No, I can't let you . . ."

"Logan, I haven't seen you in four years. My best friend has come back from the dead. You expect me to just abandon you? No, man. It doesn't matter what happens to me. You're my friend, and friends support each other. No matter what."

He was so astonished by this act of loyalty, he forgot all about his drink. "I'm sorry for leaving."

"Don't be. I probably would have gone crazy too. I'm just glad to know you're alive, man."

"Thanks, Tom." He brought up his hand, clasping Tom's into an old, familiar handshake. "You really are the best of friends."

He shrugged. "I try. By the way, I think I know where we need to go." He got up from his chair and loomed over Logan. "Follow me."

Chapter 17

"What? Where?" Logan asked, surprised.

Tom rolled his eyes. "Dude, just trust me."

He did. He got up from his seat, the chair squeaking as it went backward. He followed Tom out the tiny door of the coffee shop and out onto the busy sidewalk, where they caught a bus at the corner. Forced to stand, they hung on to the hand rails, jolting back and forth.

"So you want to tell me where we're going?" Logan asked as his shoes slid across the black floor.

"We're going to a house."

"Oh, really helpful."

Tom smiled. "Okay. We're going to see an old friend."

"An old friend? My friend or yours?"

"Both."

"Hmm." He thought back to the friends they had in common. It had to be someone from either church or college. He couldn't think of anyone who stood out as having a place of refuge for two people trying to combat Satan and stop the apocalypse.

Although, that wasn't an easy description to fit.

"Kim?"

"Nope."

"Kyle?"

"No."

"I bet its Ben. Is it Ben?"

He laughed. "Dude seriously, you're going to have to wait until we get there."

Logan smiled. He was mostly just trying to keep the conversation light. It was hard, especially when the events of the day trickled back into his memory.

After what seemed an eternity, the bus began to slow down. Tom indicated that this was their stop. Logan wasn't sure where they were at. The buildings were composed of cracked brick, and down the road was an old opera house with white pillars, which didn't look like it had been used in a long time. On the left side, there were several local businesses. Broken down antique stores, gift shops, bookstores with broken signs. He had lived in New York his whole life. How did he not recognize this neighborhood?

"I haven't been in these parts too often either," Tom said, as if reading his thoughts. "This part of the city hasn't been modernized."

"No kidding."

They climbed out as the bus rolled to a stop. It was getting darker by the second, the purple light almost sunken over the top of the buildings.

"We'd better get moving," Tom breathed.

They quickened their pace across the cracked sidewalk, their path lit by the last rays of sun and a few dim street lamps.

Logan hoped that Tom knew where they were going. Fortunately, he seemed to. He led him for two blocks then took a right, entering a dark street lined with brick houses. Logan found himself glancing back every few steps, certain he saw a figure standing within the shadows.

Finally, they came upon a tall, skinny house made of tan-colored brick. Its gray roof came at a dramatic slant. Its two large windows were lined with white panels, and flowers dotted the sides of the house. Tom led him up the concrete steps to a porch that was riddled with garden materials. A familiar scent tickled Logan's nostrils.

Tom rapped sharply on the door. They waited for several moments before they detected faint footsteps approaching from inside. After another minute, the door swung open. Logan couldn't believe who he was seeing.

Her name was Sophia Parks. She had attended church with the both of them many years ago, and she had always been one of Logan's favorite people. She was old and wise, with a large grin and a quirky sense of humor. In her inflection, one might think they were her favorite person in the world, but her eyes were a deep pool of mystery.

He remembered that smell. Sophia had always had a particular scent, like a mix of peppermint and roses.

She clutched onto the door, her blue eyes locked on Logan. Her lips parted in shock.

"Hi Sophia!" Tom greeted.

"Logan Lokte," she breathed. "Is that really you?"

Even in her old age, her voice rung like a bell.

"It's really me," he replied.

Stunned, she embraced him, her frail arms wrapping lightly around him.

"I heard you were dead," she said quietly.

"You heard wrong."

She let him go. Her wispy gray hair was down, framing her sunken face and dropping loose hairs on her white cardigan. She huddled back to the door, where she continued to survey him like an inspector.

"Hey, you haven't seen me in a while either," Tom said with a hint of frustration.

"I knew where you were. I didn't know what happened to Logan." Her eyes finally went to Tom. "But don't think I'm not happy to see you."

He smiled.

"Gentlemen, as great as it is to see both of you, I have a feeling you didn't come here to say hi. What can I do for you?"

"We were actually wondering if we could stay here a few nights," Logan said tentatively.

She blinked in surprise. "Well, sure. Did you lose your apartment, Tom?"

"Oh no, no. It's just, there are things that we need to talk about that my roommates really aren't ready to hear. And we don't have much money for a hotel. So, I figured, if anyone could understand . . ."

"It would be me," she finished. Her eyebrows were pulled together curiously, but she did not inquire further. "Well then, I suppose you two should come inside."

They did. Logan's eyes traced the floor and ceiling. The floors were made of a dark, worn hardwood, with a welcome mat in front of the door. The walls were lined with floral wallpaper, extending into the kitchen and along a staircase that winded into an upstairs. She led them into the living room. It was intimate, with no television and a large brick fireplace in the center, surrounded by a wall of books. The furniture was antique but comfortable, with a floral design and a small wooden coffee table scattered with old newspapers. She did not seem embarrassed by the clutter. She led them into the room and offered a kind smile.

"Can I get you boys anything from the kitchen?"

They both asked for a water, and she hobbled out. They looked at each other. This was their chance to talk privately, with no one to judge them. But now that they were there, they were at loss for words.

"Logan," Tom finally began, his gaze directed towards the hardwood. "How do you plan to save her?"

". . . I don't know. I guess I'll just have to trust that God will show me how."

A moment later, Sophia came in with two full glasses of water. She sat down across from them and leaned forward.

"I have opened my house to the both of you," she said. "Now I ask for answers."

They looked at each other again. She was certainly kind and open-minded . . . but could she really understand?

"It all started when Jasmine passed," Logan said.

He told her the same story he told Tom; his encounters with the devil, his change, his years of servitude to Satan, and his meeting Marianne. When he was done, Sophia did not have the look of amazement that Tom had. Instead, she leaned back on the cushion, gazing ahead thoughtfully.

". . . It seems you have had a hard few years, Logan. I'm truly sorry."

He was taken aback. Why was everyone sorry? Why didn't they judge him, like he judged himself?

Instead of expressing this wonder, he smiled. "Thank you."

She placed her hands in her lap. "So what now? What's your plan?"

"Woah," Tom interjected. "I knew you had experience with this type of stuff, but you seriously don't have any questions about that story? You don't doubt it even a little bit?"

She smiled an aged smile. "Thomas, when you have lived as long as I have, and seen as much as I've seen, you learn that there is so much beyond what is in front of us. Believe it or not, this is not the craziest truth I've heard in my lifetime."

He opened his mouth to reply, then closed it again.

"So what is your plan?" she asked.

Logan sighed. "I don't know. I guess tomorrow we can check all the places she would go. Her house, her work, her church. I'll see if I can find her and talk to her."

"Yeah, because that worked so well last time," Tom muttered.

"If you have any better ideas, I'd be happy to hear them."

"I just know that this isn't the same girl you knew. I don't think talking is going to work."

"Well I've got to do something."

"I think Logan's right," Sophia said. "All you can do is talk to her, and allow her to make the decision from there. God's the only one who can help her now."

He nodded solemnly. "And if I can, I need to keep her from committing any more murders."

"That would be the hard part," she commented.

"Yes. But if I can just . . ."

At that moment, there was a loud crack that thundered throughout the house. The window behind them shattered, and they ducked down onto the floor. Four more shots rang out, the cracks deafening, swift bullets striking the floral walls. Logan pressed his hands against his ears, his forehead touching the hardwood. He didn't have time for fear, only confusion. Where were these gunshots coming from?

The shots stopped, and Logan could hear the screeching of tires as a car sped away outside. The three of them lifted their heads. None of them were injured, but the bullets had torn through the window, the wall, and bits of the antique furniture.

They looked at one another silently for a moment.

Tom stumbled around the room and yelled. "What the hell was that?!"

Chapter 18

Marianne walked along the sidewalk, Logan's image brewing in her mind.

The ignorant coward. Who did he think he was dealing with? Breaking a deal with their Master . . . and right after she signed the contract! What was his motive? What force compelled him to commit mutiny during to onset of the apocalypse? To abandon his mission, the demon that provided him power . . .

To abandon her.

It doesn't matter, the demon of vengeance growled.

Of course, the demon was right. Her petty feelings only mattered when she was human. She was so much more now, so above every living thing, including Logan. She hadn't planned on seeing him again, anyway. He was simply a means to an end, a way to attain what she wanted in life. Now he was just a nuisance. A stupid, handsome nuisance.

She pushed past a cuddling couple who shot her angry glares. If only they knew. They wouldn't look at her with any expression but fear. She could turn back now, if she wanted. Teach them some respect. She could snap both their necks and not have wasted a second of her time.

But it wasn't worth the effort. They would be dead soon. Until then, she had to focus her efforts on vengeance. Simple death was not good enough for the people who had ruined the past two years of her life. They would die in agonizing pain as the light faded from their eyes. Their screams would echo through the streets until their voices were too weak to let out another sound.

Much like Christopher Ballard. Such a thrill, breaking every bone in his body before finally sending a knife into his stomach. His screams had seemed to go on for hours.

Now it was time for her next victim. She pivoted, gazing with a smile at the building with a sea of potential prey inside.

The daycare.

"Gunshots." Logan grunted. "Someone was shooting at us."

"Well, obviously," Tom replied. "But why? A drive-by, maybe?"

Sophia was on her feet within seconds. "No, Tom. I think we all know that this was not a coincidence."

Both pairs of eyes turned to Logan. He held his hands up defensively. "What, are you saying Marianne had something to do with this?" When they were silent, his gaze narrowed. "No way."

Tom took a step forward. "Oh come on, Logan! That woman hung a dead man to her ceiling with barbed wire, then knocked us down three flights of stairs. I don't think she's beyond shooting at us."

"But it doesn't make any sense!" Logan put an aggravated hand to his forehead. "Her murder of Ballard was detailed, elaborate. This is the demon of *vengeance* we're talking about. If she wanted to kill me, she would make it artistic. She wouldn't just shoot at me and drive away."

"Dude, did you just call murder artistic?"

Sophia held up a hand to silence them. "No matter who it was, I believe we can all agree that from here, we should exercise caution. You boys are going to help me board up the windows and barricade the doors."

"With all due respect, I think I'm just going to leave."

The two looked at Logan critically.

"Look, you both could have died just now, and it's all my fault. I'm pretty sure that, whoever it is, they're after me, not you. I don't want to put you into any more danger."

Sophia's face suddenly turned gentle. She approached Logan, laying a comforting hand on his shoulder. "No, son. I am not about to let you put yourself in harm's way."

"But . . ."

"No. Your parents have been in a fit wondering what happened to you. And now that you're in my home, it's my duty to keep you safe. If you don't stay alive for yourself, do it for your parents. Okay?"

He felt his heart sink. He had hardly had the time to consider how his disappearance affected his family. Just one more thing to feel guilty about.

". . . Alright, fine. For them. But we are going to barricade this house. And while we do, we're going to come up with a plan to save Marianne."

They agreed. They were still shaky from their near-death experience moments prior, and they found themselves ducking as they passed the living room window. Sophia led them to furnished basement where tools, lumber, and engineering equipment lay stacked in huge pile in the corner. From a distance, it looked like scrap metal and garbage.

"This should be just about everything you'll need," she commented as they rummaged through the mess. "My husband used to stock up for the apocalypse, he did. I always thought he was crazy for it. Now I guess I'm the crazy one."

Her husband . . . Logan had never met her husband in life, but she had certainly talked about him enough. He knew he was a man of great faith. He loved the city, but also loved vacationing in the countryside. He enjoyed building things and cooking. He hardly ever let Sophia have a hand in the kitchen.

Logan didn't know what happened to him. He assumed he must have died many years ago.

They took the tools they needed and trudged back up the wooden staircase. In the living room, they boarded the window, covering every inch until there was no more light, and not even the smallest breeze crept through the cracks. They talked about the shooting, the conversation seeming to go in circles until the topic finally steered.

"Thomas, are you still a cook down at Darren's Palace?" Sophia was sitting down on a light blue chair, a cup of hot tea held in her hand.

"I actually quit that job six months ago. I'm working at Ed's Mexican Grill, now."

"How's that going for you?" Logan asked as he tested the lumber. The nails did the trick. It held firmly in place.

"Terrible. I'm really bad at following orders."

At that moment, a memory flashed through Logan's mind. He remembered Jerry from two years ago. He was a man with a strong will, determined to push away Logan's demonic temptations.

He was bad at following orders, too. But he did. In the end, he signed that contract like everyone else. Now he was probably off somewhere, performing all sorts of evil, while a sinister demon corrupted his body and soul. All because Logan told him to . . .

He forced the thought away.

"You know, you should open up your own restaurant," Logan muttered, attempting to force down the guilt. "You always wanted to."

"I know. It's my dream, but it's so hard. New restaurants hardly ever succeed in this city."

"I think yours would," Sophia chirped.

"That's because you're biased."

"No, it's because you are an honest, hardworking man. And with that, you can't fail."

He smiled. "Thanks."

Logan could feel irritation creeping in. What was he doing? Sitting there, partaking in useless conversation when he should be searching for Marianne. She was out there, a demon using up her body like a parasite. The longer it remained, the darker her soul would become, and the more people she would murder.

But he could not leave now. It was the middle of the night, and whoever sent the bullets into Sophia's house could still be out there. No, he would have to wait until the morning. Should he ask Tom and Sophia what time they should leave?

No, there was no reason for them to get involved further. They were just bystanders. He could not risk their lives again.

He would sneak out in the morning.

Chapter 19

Logan woke up just as the sun settled into the sky. He shot up. He had planned on leaving before dawn. What time was it? Was anyone else awake?

He tore off the thick comforter and tip toed towards the bedroom door. Sophia had two extra bedrooms in her house, which worked out perfectly for Tom and Logan. It had been musty, like the bed had not been occupied for years, but it was comfortable.

He opened the door, which creaked on rusty hinges. He peered around the upstairs hallway. All was silent. The doors were closed, and the only light came from a single lamp that sent dim rays from downstairs. He walked towards the staircase, careful to step lightly on the floor. The lamp's light became brighter as he got closer. It illuminated the front door, where Marianne lay somewhere on the other side.

He approached the door, gazing at the long line of locks. He proceeded to open them, the metal rattling under his grip. One lock . . . two locks . . . only three more . . .

The fourth padlock slipped and landed with a crash on the hardwood.

Silence, then shuffling upstairs.

He forced the final lock out and flung the door open. A bright morning sun shone through. He rushed out and bounded down the sidewalk.

"LOGAN?!" Tom called from behind.

Logan turned to face him. He was caught. There was no point in running.

Tom's shirt flapped loosely in the wind. "Dude, what are you doing?"

"I'm going after Marianne, and you can't come with me."

Tom's eyes narrowed. "Why not?"

"I don't want you getting hurt," he said. "Besides, you'll just slow me down."

He expected Tom to yell at him. Instead, his eyes were filled with something that resembled both contempt and pity. "Logan . . . you need to stop."

"What do you mean?"

"You need to stop this pursuit of Marianne."

Logan took a step back. ". . . I thought you were behind me?"

"I am, but not if you insist on doing this. It's not good for you, man. It's only going to lead to more heartbreak."

Logan could feel his insides starting to boil. "Seriously, Tom? What are you saying, that you want me to let these murders happen? To allow the start of the apocalypse?"

"This isn't about the apocalypse!" Tom said, his voice rising. "You're doing this because you want to be a hero, save the girl, sweep her off her feet. But life doesn't work that way. Some people can't be saved."

"Okay, let me get this straight. You want me to just abandon all these victims? To abandon Marianne? To leave her a slave to Satan, like I was?"

"Yes. It's a lost cause, Logan."

"I don't care if it's a lost cause or not. I love her!"

"You don't love her!" Tom said, his words pouring like a tidal wave. "You just think you love her because she looks like Jasmine!"

Logan stopped. Tom looked down, his cheeks flushing red. "I'm sorry, but it's true."

"She . . . she doesn't look like Jasmine."

"You haven't noticed? Really think about it, and tell me she doesn't."

He did, and he realized that Tom was right. They had different complexions, but they were alike in every other way. Full, pink lips, long, angular noses. Petite, toned bodies and narrow eyes. They even had similar voices.

He suddenly wondered what had drawn him to Marianne in the first place.

"Okay, so maybe a little bit," Logan said. "But what does that matter?"

"It matters because you're seeing Marianne as something she's not. You're seeing her as your dead wife, and now that she's slipping away, you're trying to save her. You're trying to save Jasmine. But she's gone, man. You have to let her go."

His heart felt like it'd been struck with a knife. He glared at Tom.

"You don't know what you're talking about."

"Yes I do." Tom said. "You don't have to be a genius to see it."

"No, I love Marianne. I love her with everything that I have. And when you love someone, you don't just get up and leave them!"

There was a moment of dead silence, the only sound being Logan's unsteady breaths. Tom's expression turned to ice.

"You're right. You don't."

Logan's anger was quickly replaced by guilt. "Look, I didn't mean . . ."

"You know what? Just go. Go be with the psychotic murderer. But when she kills you, don't come crying to me beyond the grave."

He started to turn away.

"Tom, wait . . ."

"For what?" he asked, cocking his head slightly. "For my best friend to come back? I've waited. I'm pretty sure he's gone."

Logan could do nothing but watch as he strolled down the street, his figure disappearing into Sophia's front door.

~~~

Tom slammed the door behind him.

What was wrong with Logan? Was he really that naïve? So infatuated by this girl, that he was blind to the fact that she was evil?

That man's dead body, hanging like a mutilated painting on her ceiling, still lingered in his mind. Logan had seen it too. Was that not enough for him to realize she was beyond saving?

He was wrong to hope that he'd changed. Logan was still a selfish, scared boy wanting to play the hero. He never listened to Tom.

Tom put his head in his hands. "Lord, please help him . . ."

"A prayer?" a sly voice echoed. "I don't see God here, do you?"

Tom jerked at the sound. Standing a few feet in front of him was a tall man with a strong jaw, glistening blonde hair and sharp blue eyes. He wore loose, dark clothes, and a small red scar lined the side of his left eye. The scar looked fresh, as if it had just been put there a few days ago.

Tom gazed at the man, his mouth agape. Had he been there the whole time?

"Who the hell are you?" the words stumbled out of his mouth.

A wicked grin flashed across his face. "Hell indeed, Thomas. I'm an old acquaintance of your friend, Logan Lokte. I am Sallos."

~~~

Logan trailed down the sidewalk, his head toward the ground. He hadn't meant to hurt Tom. He just didn't want to put him in unnecessary danger. Not to mention, Tom had wanted him to give up his pursuit of Marianne. That was something he couldn't do.

Though, he was right about one thing. Marianne did resemble Jasmine, so much that it was frightening.

Cars zoomed by, blowing cool air against his body. He wasn't sure where to go. Marianne said she wanted revenge. Where would that take her? To the theaters that rejected her, maybe? To her old church? The truth was, he hadn't known her long enough to have a solid idea.

He looked up at the sky. "God, please help me," he muttered under his breath. "Show me where to go."

A small shadow flickered across the beaming sun. He blinked. As his eyes adjusted, he caught the sight of a white dove, flying swiftly across the sky. It dived, swooping down just a few feet in front of him. He stepped back. It flew up again, perching on a lamp post across the street. It then craned its neck towards him, its black eyes boring into his.

This has to be a coincidence, he thought. It was just a bird, right? But as he stared back at the creature, he heard the sound of a bell. His eyes trailed downward. The dove had landed in front of an elementary school. Children were going inside, backpacks hoisted over their little shoulders.

Children. The daycare.

"... Thank you."

He bounded across the sidewalk.

~~~

Marianne strapped on a loose apron as she walked towards the daycare. Coming up with a story on why she hadn't been at work all week was too easy.

"I'm so sorry," she had said, crying fake tears over the phone. "It's just, m-my mother was back in the hospital, and they said she wasn't going to make it . . . I just had to fly back home. I-I'm sorry I didn't tell you before. I've just been so scared, I didn't think . . ."

"Oh Marianne, don't worry about it. I completely understand," her boss replied. "Take all the time you need."

"No . . . I want to come back. I want to come back to work, please."

She could almost see her boss giving a stupid, sympathetic smile. "Of course you can."

"Oh, thank you! Thank you so much!"

She wanted to laugh at her gullibility.

Now she was here, walking into that dreadful daycare. She could already hear a screaming child inside.

Children. She used to love them. Now she hated them. They had only brought her down these past two years. Selfish little heathens, running around with no care in the world. So dependent upon other people to survive, and simply expecting them to fill these needs. Creatures driven only by their own desire. Much like her, really, only they were too naïve to realize their own vanity.

And unlike them, she had power.

She put on a sad face as she walked in. One of her coworkers came up to her, and she formed a fake, weary smile.

"Marianne," her coworker said. "I'm so sorry about your mother. Is she okay?"

She let out a dramatic sigh. "Still the same. People keep saying I should just pull the plug . . . but I don't know if I'm ready yet. You know?"

She nodded. "Of course. You just lay back today, alright? Take it easy."

"Thanks, but that won't be necessary. I need some normalcy right now. Even if that means throwing myself into a pack of crazy children."

She smiled. "I understand. You look great today, by the way."

Marianne looked down at her outfit. It was true, she wasn't exactly dressed for a daycare. She was sporting black skinny jeans and tall, shiny black heels. Her shirt was a loose tank top dotted with red and black, and her long black hair was fashioned gracefully on each side rather than being thrown up in a bun. She wasn't stupid. She knew when she was getting dressed that she might stand out among her colleagues. But ever since the change, she had an increased realization of the power of sexuality. For some women, it was their undoing. For her, it was a tool.

She smiled politely. "Thank you."

Toddlers continued to show up. The ones who could talk recognized her instantly, exclaiming her name and showering her with hugs.

Disgusting.

"Ms. Marianne, what's that black stuff on your eyes?" one little girl asked, her curly blonde hair pulled back in a long, swinging ponytail.

Marianne forced a smile. "Its eyeliner, sweetheart."

"It looks funny," she said with a giggle.

Marianne frowned. She imagined her hands settling around the girl's weak little head. Twisting it around in one violent stroke, easy as turning a bottle cap on a soda . . .

She shook the thought away. She had to be patient. Wait until the end of the day. Then she could have her fun.

"Mari!" A desperate voice sounded out.

She turned around. Standing in the doorway was Logan Lokte. He was a mess. His dark brown hair was tussled unevenly around his defined cheeks, and his clothes were baggy, as if he had been too rushed to get dressed that morning. She couldn't help but snicker. The betrayer, still pursuing her like a lost stray. Pathetic.

He approached her, his lips set in a fine line on his face.

She was the first to speak. "Well, well, if it isn't God's little pawn. Tell me, how's life as a slave working out for you?"

"You're the slave, not me."

"Actually, I am freer than ever before."

He paused, his dark eyes searching hers. ". . . We need to talk."

"Well I'm right here, knight of the heavenly table. Talk away."

He apparently expected a less warm welcome, because he took a minute to respond. "Why . . . why are you working at the daycare?"

"Oh, you know I just *love* children!" The sarcasm was thick in her voice.

He smiled slightly. "I had a demon in me once too, you know. I know you hate children now."

"What a keen observation. You should be a detective."

She moved forward, her six inch heels gliding across the floor.

"Marianne, you have to stop this," he said. "It's not you. I know you think it is, but it's not. All these thoughts you are having are not your own. I didn't realize it either. I didn't realize I was trapped until . . . well, until I met you."

His words sent a sudden rush of feeling through her.

Don't forget what he did to you Marianne, the demon hissed. *He's a filthy, lying traitor. There is no room for forgiveness in vengeance, my dear.*

Yes, vengeance and destruction. That was what she was. She could not stray from it.

"And yet you still had me sign the deal." She started to turn away. "Some man of God you are . . ."

He grasped onto her arm. "I did it to save your life!"

She gazed into his earnest eyes. "What?"

"Lucifer didn't like how long I was waiting to turn you. She said that if I didn't get it done, you would be killed. I see now that I made a mistake. But I did it all to save you."

She was taken aback. Had allowing her to sign away her soul actually been an act of love? A twinge of happiness fluttered in her heart. The demon cringed.

This conversation was delving into dangerous territory. She could not afford to be having human feelings. Not now.

Marianne placed her mouth by his ear, speaking in a low whisper. "I don't care what you have or haven't done for me, Logan Lokte. I have signed a contract and, unlike you, I choose to fulfill it. As soon as you leave, I will take one of these children, and I will rip them apart. You cannot stop me. And if you try . . . well, let's just say that forgiveness is not in my nature."

She drew her face back and relished his fearful expression.

"What are you doing?" she exclaimed suddenly, causing several pairs of eyes to turn to her. "Get your hand off of me!"

That handsome face was put into stupid confusion. "What?"

"Please, let me go. Stop. HELP! SOMEONE, HELP!"

He withdrew his hand as her coworkers rushed to her side.

"What's going on, Marianne?" one girl asked.

She pointed a shaking hand at Logan. "T-This man was trying to hurt me!"

His eyes narrowed, his veins beginning to showcase in his arms. He was adorable when he was angry. "I was not, and you know it!"

"Sir, I am calling the police right now," one woman said. "I suggest that you leave."

He pushed back against a row of women who stood defensively in front of Marianne. "Don't shut me out, Mari. I know you're in there."

She continued to make a fake crying face until her coworker's gazes were averted. As they pushed Logan towards the door, she let a small smile form on the corner of her lips and shot him a dramatic wink. He shouted her name before being shoved on the cold, hard sidewalk.

Good riddance.

Chapter 20

Logan fell over his own feet, his tailbone striking the sidewalk. The sound of police sirens rung out in the distance. The passing people on the sidewalk glanced down at him before scurrying away.

He forced himself up. He had to leave before the police arrived. He walked briskly, his hands shoved in his pockets as he weaved through the passing crowds. The sirens were getting closer, and it was hard not to break into a run.

After walking almost a block, he turned into a nearby store. He was greeted by a smiling employee.

"Hello sir," the man said, the lines on his face lighting up. "Is there anything I can help you find?"

Logan was too stressed to fake a smile. "No, I'm just looking."

"Alright, well take your time sir, and please let me know if you need anything."

He replied with a nod and walked ahead. He was in a souvenir shop. The aisles were lined with assorted New York trinkets; magnets, calendars, postcards, t-shirts. The fluorescent lights lit up the store, shining off the merchandise and giving them a bright, almost harsh look. He walked down one of the narrow aisles. He leaned against the metal and sighed, allowing his eyes to close.

He had tried to talk, and Marianne rejected him instantly. Now she planned on killing an innocent child. It seemed he had no way of stopping her . . .

He looked up towards the ceiling, trying to fight the tears that threatened to spill from his eyes.

What now?

Cold fear trickled down Tom's spine. There was no humanity reflected in Sallos' gaze. It reminded him of when he saw Marianne, that mix of indifference and amusement . . .

He swallowed dryly. "An old acquaintance, you said?"

Sallos smiled. "Yes. Before he decided to become a weakling."

He advanced towards him, and Tom found himself pressed against the wall. He grabbed uncertainly at the plaster. Was there a weapon anywhere? A knife? Anything? There was a poker by the fireplace, but that was past Sallos and beyond his reach.

"So, when Logan was a demon?" he stalled. "That must have been interesting."

"Not really. He was kind of dull." He chuckled. "He didn't like the way I killed people."

Tom ran towards the door. He threw himself against it, placing a hand on the metal handle and yanking it open . . .

Sallos grabbed him by the hair. Before he could fight back, he flung him on the ground. His body skidded against the hardwood. Pain shot up his shoulder. Sallos shut the door, pacing in front of it casually.

"You know, I thought he would have gotten the message when I shot those bullets through the window. But he was still insistent on pursuing this love nonsense. Now, because of him, I have to kill you."

Tom hands were shaking. He muttered the thing he could think to say: "Why?"

This appeared to amuse him. "Why? Because, insolent boy, this is not just about a single soul. This is the apocalypse. Lucifer is not about to lose her most vital weapon just because of some love-sick child, is she?" He pulled a long dagger out of his slacks. It was jagged and worn, as if it had been used many times before. "And unfortunately for you, you chose the wrong side."

Tom backed up against the wall, his shoulder throbbing. He could do nothing as those eyes bore into him hungrily.

"I do wish Logan could be here to see this," Sallos mused. "I had hoped to kill you both together. Oh well. He will find out soon enough."

Tom forced his eyes shut and waited for the dagger to pierce his chest.

But it never came. Instead, loud, maniacal laughter resounded through the house, echoing off the walls. He opened his eyes.

Standing in front of a laughing Sallos was Sophia. She held a large, wooden cross, her chin raised. She stared at the demon with a radiating confidence that made Tom think she had done this before. Sallos tucked the dagger back in his pants.

"In the name of Christ our Lord," she seethed, her small lips parted into a scowl. "I command you to leave!"

This only made Sallos laugh harder. "You pathetic old woman! Do you honestly think that a little cross and a few words are going to banish me? I'm not one of the weak little demons you are used to exorcising."

Tom took the opportunity to inch up the wall, standing on shaking legs.

Sophia shoved the cross nearer to his face. He flinched. "Every demon can be banished in the name of God. Now I command you, in the name of Christ Jesus, leave this place!"

A flicker of fear flashed across Sallos' face, giving Tom hope that he may leave after all. But the fear vanished in an instant, replaced by cold arrogance. He snatched cross, his hands sizzling on the metal and sending trails of smoke to the ceiling. Uncertainty filled in her eyes as she stared at that cruel smile.

"You see, Sophia Parks, I am not a fragile demon fighting to possess some mortal. I am the demon of chaos. And if there is one thing in this world that is constant, it is chaos."

Just as his hands seemed that they were about to burn away, he threw the cross on the ground. He grabbed Sophia by the throat, holding her up so that her feet dangled above the ground. Her milky eyes were wide with fear as he tossed her against the opposite wall, forcing her hunched body against the plaster. She landed by the fireplace, blood pouring from the top of her head.

He held out his arms dramatically. "You just can't get rid of me!"

Tom stepped forward. If he could just get the knife, which was gleaming from Sallos' slacks . . .

Sallos gazed back at him. "You know I'd break your neck before you could even try."

He stopped in his tracks.

Sallos moved towards Sophia, strolling by the fireplace and staring indifferently at her broken body. He reached down and turned on a switch, causing the fireplace to roar with life. His eyes blazed like the fire.

"You know," he said. "I'm glad you're the one to go first. You are quite the pest."

He grabbed the fireplace poker, turning it lightly in his hand before placing the end in the fire. It burned bright orange. "Not that you could have hurt me."

Even in her mangled state, Sophia managed to speak, her voice stifled. "There is . . . a time f-for everything. A time to be born . . . and a time to die." Sallos leaned towards her as she spoke. ". . . It is my time to die."

"You know what I think?" The poker burned hot in his hand. "I think God used you. Your whole life was spent in service of this big, celestial being. You'd think He'd at least let you die with a little dignity. But instead, you're going to die here, bones broken and at the hands of a demon. Now what kind of God would let you die like that? Wouldn't He at least try to save you?" He looked up towards the ceiling with a mocking smile. "Come on God! I'm standing right here. If you have any objection to this, come down and save your faithful servant! Smite me with fire!"

All was silent.

Sallos leaned down and whispered into her ear. "You see? He doesn't care."

A single tear ran down her cheek. Sallos stood up and reared back his arm, where the poker blazed in his hand. Sophia's gaze trickled up to Tom's.

"Run, Tom," she choked.

Sallos peered at his rigid form and smiled cruelly. "Yes, Tom. If I were you, I would run."

He reared back the poker further. Tom stumbled out the front door just as the hot poker bore down into Sophia's chest.

~~~

Logan didn't know what to do.

If he wanted to save the child, he had to go back to the daycare. But the thought filled him with dread. After all, what could he possibly do to stop her? He didn't have demon-like strength anymore. What chance did he have? Talking was off the table, and he was too weak to try to use force. The child was probably just as likely to survive if he didn't interfere at all.

He resisted the urge to sink down onto the store's dirty tile. Maybe he just wasn't cut out for the job. The apocalypse was inevitable anyways, right? Perhaps he should have gone home and seen his parents one last time before the chaos ensued. Even if it meant losing Marianne . . .

The thought stabbed him like a million knives, and he found himself leaning on his knees, his teeth gritted in agony. How could he even think that? He couldn't give up on the woman he loved. She was still in there, a prisoner buried beneath a demon. It was his fault she had ended up there in the first place. He couldn't lose her . . .

Not again.

He grimaced at the thought. Perhaps Tom was right. Perhaps he was trying to save Jasmine.

So what if he was? Whether this was about Jasmine or not, he had still known Marianne. She was a good person. He may not have been able to save her, but she deserved a man who would try. If there was an ounce of goodness in his soul, he would at least attempt to fix this mess he created.

He bowed his head in a silent prayer. "God, please protect me and be with me. Give me the right actions and words to say. Please guide me down the right path."

As he lifted his head, he could not fight the twinge of guilt that stabbed his heart. Sometimes he did not feel right speaking to God after all he had done.

He mustered up all the strength within him to get his weak legs working. He charged through the store and out the door, his head in a daze. The sun bore on his face. He could not go through the front of the daycare. Not this time. He would have to sneak around the back. Once he did that, he would try to apprehend Marianne. If he could not, he may at least force her to expose what she truly was. Then the kids may have a chance.

He could see the cracked building clear in the daylight. The police were just leaving, parked behind a silver sports car. There was no action for them there. Not yet, anyways.

He approached the one-story block of stone, moving towards the small alleyway that separated it from its neighboring building. Behind the daycare was a playground. Small, with only two slides and a swing set. He traveled the alleyway and turned towards the back of the building, his feet trudging lightly against playground pebbles. On the back of the building a red door stood before him, steady and bright as the sun. He placed his hand on the handle . . .

"What's my surprise?" a little girl's voice echoed through the doorway.

Two pairs of footsteps were approaching. He stopped.

"Hush, now." It was Marianne. "Patience is a virtue."

They were getting closer. He rushed from the doorway, hiding near the side of the building just as they broke through the door. He peeked from around the stone. He could see Marianne in plain view, her hawk eyes glancing back as she shut the door behind her. The child stood at her side, long hair in pig tails, wide blue eyes staring from thick rimmed spectacles. The girl grabbed tightly onto the edge of her little white dress. She had no idea the monster standing beside her.

"I don't see anything out here, Ms. Marianne," the child pouted.

"Oh not to worry, darling. Your surprise is just behind the slide."

The girl smiled and started to move forward. Logan saw a glimmer at Marianne's side; a dagger. He could not sneak up on her, not with pebbles to announce his presence. He knelt down towards the grass, his fingers forming around a large, jagged rock.

The child looked behind the slide, and Marianne unsheathed the dagger. She muttered things under her breath that Logan could not hear from where he was standing. When the girl finally turned around, she gazed in horror at Marianne's cruel face. There was nothing in those dark eyes, only pure, unsolicited evil. She raised the knife triumphantly, and a scream erupted from the girl's throat. Marianne started to bring the knife down . . .

Logan loosened the rock from his grip, throwing it at the back of Marianne's head. It struck her, and blood poured from her skull. She dropped the knife into the pebbles.

The girl ran away sobbing. Her pigtails flew behind her as she charged through the door.

Marianne reached to feel the wound. Red stained her fingers.

"I warned you, Logan," she whispered. "Mercy is not in my nature."

He tried to ignore the fear that was coursing through him. "Well it is in mine. I was not about to let you hurt that innocent girl."

She turned towards him in a flash. Her face was ravenous as she stomped forward, her teeth bared in a snarl. He had not taken but two steps back before she clasped her hand tightly around his throat and lifted him off his feet. He felt his windpipe start to close.

"No one is innocent!" she screamed.

He gasped for breath, but no air entered his lungs. Black spots began to enter his vision. For one brief and terrifying moment, he thought he may die.

She let go as soon as she heard footsteps bounding through the daycare. She gazed behind her, irritation on her beautiful face.

"It appears we're going to be interrupted. Not to worry, Logan. We will finish this soon."

She moved past him, her body seeming to glide along the grass until she disappeared into the bustling streets. He struggled to sit up, his hand clutched around his aching throat. He had only just gotten to his feet when the door swung open.

"Marianne? MARIANNE?!" her coworker's voice shouted into the sky. The little girl was with her, hiding behind her leg and clutching onto her jeans, as if the fabric could protect her from the world.

It was Logan's turn to go. Before they could peer around the corner of the building, he bolted, towards the sidewalk. Clusters of people brushed past him, and he searched for any sign of Marianne on the city street.

She was gone.

Chapter 21

Marianne cursed under her breath as she peeled onto the busy street, nearly hitting a black SUV and receiving angry gestures from the driver. She could have struck him and killed him, for all she cared. What she did care about, was that her task was incomplete. Thanks to Logan, her revenge on the children proved unsuccessful, and her cover was blown. Thanks to Logan, the police would soon be sniffing down her back. She wasn't afraid of them, but the fact that she could no longer stay in her own apartment perturbed her.

And I just decorated the ceiling! Despite her aggravation, she smiled at the thought.

The car she had stolen was a beauty; a sleek, silver sports car with colored headlights and a v-8 engine. Her inhuman strength broke the lock in an instant, and she had been able to start the car just by willing it. She wondered what else she could do. It was not like she had much time to test her limits. She was on a schedule, which Logan had compromised.

Curse him! If only she'd killed him before. He was so infuriating, him and his love-sick boy routine . . . what was he playing at, anyway? Was this to get back at her for rejecting his advances? It had to be. Religious facades were always driven by selfish motive. Whether it was to ease one's loneliness, justify their actions, or impress those around them, religion was always self-serving.

She took a quick right onto a small neighborhood road. The houses on each side were quaint and the yards were yellowing, a sign of the summer approaching. Chain link fences flew past her, dogs barked. She was driving fast. She soared over bumps, cracks in the pavement that were likely to never be repaired. She only had today to finish this job. How was she to do it?

That is when she saw him. Up ahead, a young boy pedaled his bike on the side of the road, long unkempt hair flying behind him. She could not see his face, but he looked to be about nine or ten years old. What was he doing out of school? What a silly question, it didn't matter. This was her chance.

No, she doubted herself. *He's too old. I've never seen this boy in my life, why him?*

But the demon reassured her. Details meant nothing, it said. It was the symbolism, the message that she would not be subdued under anyone again. So what if she didn't know him? He was still a child, and they were all the same. He deserved to live no more than the hellions that subdued her at the daycare.

She was on a schedule.

She pressed harder on the gas, until her foot seemed to be touching the floorboard. The child appeared unaware of her at first, his gaze set straight ahead and his feet flying in circles. But as she continued to gain speed, and she chunked the wheel in his direction, he turned. His mouth dropped for a split second, his big brown eyes wide with fear.

She hit him with a brute force that rattled the car and sent his little body flying over the hood. Blood smeared the windshield. He fell limply on the pavement behind her, red pouring from his chest and sinking into the cracks on the road. His eyes were open, still filled with that look of pure terror.

There was no room for guilt here. She drove on, leaving the small body and the crushed bicycle. She turned on her windshield wipers. They sprayed water and moved along the glass, but the blood only spread further, blocking her vision with a dark red blanket. It was time to steal another car.

~~~

Logan graced the steps to Marianne's apartment. Shadows fell along the wallpaper, a beam of sun providing the only light through a single window. It only took a matter of seconds to reach that familiar door. It was tall and unmoving, a haunting memory of the past weeks. He recalled Marianne, pure and innocent, with a laugh that lit up her face, her cheeks glowing a light caramel. He remembered her stepping out of that door the night of the banquet. Her beautiful yellow dress, her smile as she approached him. Less than two weeks later, it seemed more like a dream than a memory.

He placed his hand on the knob. It was unlocked- she really wasn't worried about intruders, was she? He stepped inside. Her apartment was how it had been the day before, clean and crisp, with a curtain pulled over the window. The droplets of blood were still on the hardwood, drying into thick, dark bubbles.

The first thing he noticed, however, was the stench. The smell of decay flooded his nostrils and made him want to gag. Behind the lacy blue curtain around her bed, a dead body was strung up on the ceiling, the blood drained from its rotting corpse.

He closed the door quickly, his shirt pulled tightly over his nose. He searched the bookshelves, the cushions, the kitchen cabinets. He wasn't sure what he was looking for; just any clue as to who her next target would be or where she might go. He doubted she had left any hard evidence of her plans, but it was worth a try.

When he had finally searched every cranny of the living room he slumped down. The apartment was turned over. The couch cushions were upheaved, the coffee table shifted, the bookshelves in disarray. In the kitchen all cabinets and drawers were open, pots and dishes scattered along the laminate countertops. Was there really any point in trying? Of course she wouldn't leave any clues. And even if she had, he had already searched the whole apartment.

Well, not all of it.

His eyes trickled to that sky blue curtain. Surely she didn't still go in that room. Or maybe she did. She was demented, after all. There were two nightstands in there that he hadn't searched. The thought of being so close to Ballard turned his stomach in knots.

There had been a time when dead bodies did not phase him. He remembered right after the demon entered him, Sallos had been excited to show him his work. He had followed him to a camping ground in upstate New York. There, five bodies lay, their tents ripped to shreds and their blood scattered along the rocks. They were still in the night, their eyes wide open. A mother, a father, and three children under the age of sixteen. Just an innocent, family camping trip.

"What is it that you do?" Logan inquired calmly.

"I create chaos," Sallos said.

"Chaos? Wouldn't that be better made with mass hysteria, rather than targeting a single family? Disease? Or a biological weapon, perhaps?"

"Oh, those are great tools. But you see, Logan, I don't need any of that. Chaos is created by fear. And what are people most afraid of?"

He acted like a teacher lecturing his student. Logan answered simply. "Death."

"Exactly. I don't have the power to create disease. But if I can make people afraid of mundane events, then I have already generated chaos. For if it is not safe to just go camping, what else isn't safe to do? Fear drives people out of their minds."

Logan turned to him, surveying Sallos' features. He was in a different body back then. He was in the form of a Middle-Eastern man with long, shaggy black hair and big brown eyes. He was stout and muscular, with handsome features and an untrimmed face. There was something strange about him. There was fire behind those eyes, harsh and unfamiliar . . .

"You're not like me, are you?"

"What do you mean?"

"There is a demon in me, but I'm still here. I still have my soul. You don't, do you?"

He smiled cruelly. "Thank the devil for that, right?"

"But how . . ?"

"Some demons require a compatible human spirit present to keep the body functioning. Your demon needs you. I, on the other hand, don't need anything but a freshly dead body to possess."

"Why are demons different like that?"

"Don't know, don't care," he replied.

A lie. He just didn't feel like explaining it. Logan was becoming quite good at detecting lies.

He gazed back at the five bodies. It had been made to look like a bear attack. Blood covered the grounds, their skin slashed all along their exposed backs and chests. The youngest was no older than twelve. He looked blankly at the sky, his open face strewn with red and his stomach torn open, revealing his insides. Logan peered at the gruesome sight for well over a minute.

He'd felt nothing.

The memory flashed through his mind as he stared at the curtain. He longed for that indifference, if only to help drive him into the room. He wondered what it was about humanity that made him squeamish around dead bodies. Perhaps it was the forced recognition of his own mortality, he thought. To look upon the dead was to see what he himself would one day become. Though, he had begun craving for death long ago.

He forced his legs forward. He followed that familiar blood trail across the room and stood in front of the lacy cloth, which he grasped with a sweaty hand. He forced the sheet open.

Ballard was there, alright. He could sense him in his peripheral, though he did not dare look up. His nose plugged and his eyes downcast, he rushed past the bed, his side brushing the comforter that was stiff with dried blood. He tore open the drawers to the left nightstand, but found only pencils and an old phonebook. One more to go. He went to the nightstand on the right.

What a waste this will be if I don't find anything, he thought grimly. But as he threw the last drawer open, a flash of gold caught his eye. He reached into the drawer and pulled out a bible, classic King James with a black leather cover and gold pages. On the bottom left side, two words were printed in glittering letters: *Marianne Garcia.*

This caught him by surprise. When he had become possessed, he threw his bible into a fireplace. It seemed odd that Marianne would allow such an item around her. He opened the leather bounding and leafed through the pages.

Hardly one biblical word was showing. The pages were all drawn on, filled with markings from a thick black sharpie. Some of the marks were unrecognizable, but one of them he could read plainly: four. The number four was scrawled across every page, the black ink leaking through the white sheets. He skimmed through the bible. 4, 4, 4, 4, 4 . . . This went on until he reached Revelations, where the number stopped. In its place there was a symbol, appearing to be a sideways 8. He knew he had seen that symbol before, perhaps in a book somewhere . . .

He heard the front door open. He turned, and a shadowy figure appeared behind the cloth. His heart pounded. Marianne would not let him live a second time. He waited, his mouth dry, clutching tightly onto the bible.

"Logan?" The shadow called out. It was a man's voice. "Logan, are you here?"

It took him a moment to recognize it. "Tom?"

He stepped out of the bedroom. Tom turned to him, a hand held over his nose. He looked awful. His arm was scraped, and sweat formed beads along his body.

"Man, why were you in there?" he sounded weary.

"I was looking for clues. Why are *you* here? I thought you were mad at me?"

He stared at him, body tense. ". . . We're in danger."

"No, I am. You aren't involved anymore."

"No, Logan, listen to me. It doesn't matter now. We were attacked."

Logan became panicked. "Who attacked you? Marianne?"

"No. He said he knew you. He said his name was Sallos."

He froze. "Sallos? Why?"

"I don't know, he's your friend, isn't he? He said something about Lucifer, and that he had already warned us with the gunshots. He . . . he killed Sophia."

His voice cracked at the last part. Logan felt his knees weaken. Sophia was dead? He couldn't wrap his brain around that. The woman who was always there for him, who seemed so wise and strong that she could live forever. It seemed impossible, yet he knew it was true. If she came in contact with Sallos, it had to be true.

And it was all his fault.

He tried desperately to keep himself composed. "How did you escape?"

"I ran."

"You ran? He didn't catch you?"

Tom paled. "I ran as he killed her. Like a coward."

". . . Look, don't torture yourself about it. Sallos is malicious and powerful. There's nothing you could have done. If anything, it's my fault."

They were silent. Logan stared ahead, the wheels in his head spinning as if on a race track. It didn't fit. Why was Sallos trying so hard to hurt him? Tom had mentioned Lucifer. If Lucifer was involved, that could only mean one thing . . .

"Satan's Assassins," he realized.

"What?"

He was not able to finish, because at that moment, there was a knock on the door. They froze. Another knock, sharp and swift. A voice called out through the block of wood.

"Marianne? Marianne, are you home? It's Ashley, your landlord."

They looked at each other.

"She can come in here," Tom whispered.

"I know. We have to hide."

"There have been some complaints about the smell coming from this apartment," the voice said. "You mind if I take a look?"

They moved quickly out of the bedroom. They looked around the space before finally running into the bathroom, locking the door behind them. They waited, the sound of their breathing echoing against the wood.

"Marianne?"

Silence.

"Alright, I'm coming in . . ."

They heard the knob turn. Footsteps against the hardwood. Short, quick breaths. Ashley was walking forward, and Logan imagined her looking around with uncertainty.

"Marianne?"

She coughed. She had obviously inhaled too deeply.

"Marianne, are you . . . what on Earth?"

Logan stiffened. She must have found the blood trail. Her steps became more calculated. The sound of her breath stopped, as if she were holding it in.

". . . Are you alright?"

The footsteps stopped. He could see it clearly; her shaking hand clasped onto the coarse fabric. The curtain ripped open on cue, and a long, bloodcurdling scream filled the apartment. He covered his ears. She ran, the door slamming with a bang behind her.

"Man, she's gonna call the police," Tom whispered hoarsely.

"I know, we're going."

They were about to leave when a flash caught the corner of Logan's eye. He turned. Lying on the hardwood, just beneath the couch, was Marianne's cellphone, the screen gleaming in the reflecting light. It was flashing with a calling number, a picture of a woman on the front.

"How did I not notice that before . . ?" he muttered entirely to himself.

"Logan, hurry! Let's go!" Tom urged, already at the doorstep.

"Yeah, okay. Sorry."

Chapter 22

They went to a motel shortly after.

It was not at all like Logan's hotel in Manhattan, with marble floors and on-hand room service. This was two stories high, with concrete pathways and a cracked, uneven parking lot. The flimsy wooden doors were on the outside of the building, which was a dirty white color, with one rusty railing guarding the second story of rooms. Inside the room were two queen beds with dark floral comforters. The walls were a plain tan, with a single dull light radiating from the ceiling. The rough carpet was stained, and the double sink outside of the bathroom sported a yellow laminate top. A small, black television stood across from their bed, its rounded screen giving him a flashback of the 90s.

Despite the condition of the hotel, Logan was grateful to Tom for paying.

"Are you sure about this?" he asked.

"Oh yeah, I have a little money put back. I was saving it for a trip, but this is more important. I can travel anytime, right?"

His tone was reassuring, but his eyes conveyed uncertainty.

They collapsed on the beds. Tom grabbed the remote next to him and began flipping through the channels. Logan skimmed through the bible, his eyes searching the number four and the strange sideways eight in Revelations.

"So what was that you were saying back there?" Tom asked. "Satan's something?"

"Satan's Assassins. That's what demons call them. They're assassins that Lucifer hires for her most important jobs. She employs her most powerful demons to kill the people she's too busy to kill herself. What gets me is how rare it is. Demons have their own purposes. Sallos is supposed to cause chaos, but it's hard for him to do that if he's busy hunting us down. She saves her assassins for special occasions, when someone is getting in the way of something important. If Sallos has been hijacked into Satan's Assassins, then we must really be pissing her off."

"What's the big deal? I mean, even if we succeeded in helping Marianne, so what? Couldn't her demon just find another body to go into?"

Logan shook his head. "No. Bodies can reject certain demons, and if the assassins are getting involved, I'd say Marianne is the only compatible body they've found. What I don't get is, why Sallos? Why the assassins? Marianne seems pretty intent on killing me herself. I don't see why they don't just let her do it."

"Maybe they don't trust her."

"Yeah, maybe."

Tom sighed. "I guess we'll have to get a different hotel each night to keep Sallos off our backs."

"Yeah, that should help, but it doesn't guarantee anything. He tracked us pretty quick to Sophia's, didn't he?"

Tom flinched at Sophia's name. Logan decided to change the subject.

"Hey, what do you suppose this symbol is?" He handed the bible to him, the page turned to Revelations.

"Not sure. It looks familiar, though."

"I know. I just can't place it."

"I can look it up. Give me a sec."

He whipped out a cell phone from his pocket and began punch his thumbs onto the screen. Of course, Logan wouldn't think to use a cell phone. When was the last time he even had a phone? He supposed he had abandoned it after the change. It was probably way out of date compared to the new technology.

His eyes flickered toward the television. The news was on, with a young blonde newscaster, a solemn look on her pampered face. On the top left of the screen was a picture of a boy. He didn't look over ten years old. He was posing for a school picture, his hair slicked to the side and glasses falling down the tip of his nose.

A cold shiver went up Logan's spine.

"Tom, can you turn up the T.V.?"

He turned up the volume.

". . . It happened just this morning, ten year-old John Peterson was riding his bike after attending his grandfather's funeral, when he was struck by a car from behind and killed on impact. Now a 2014 silver Camaro was found parked at the intersection of 4th and Grand, just blocks from the scene, blood on the window. Another car near the area was reported stolen today, a 2012 black Sunfire with the license plate number 837-BEA. If anyone has any information related to the accident, or has seen this car, please call the number on the screen."

"A silver Camaro . . ." Logan thought back to the daycare. Hadn't there been a silver Camaro parked outside? "Marianne . . ."

"Dude, you've got to let me in on what you're talking about."

He looked up at Tom. "Marianne killed that boy."

"She killed him? Why? I thought she just wanted to kill the kids at her work?"

"I thought so too . . ." He peered at the screen again, which was just changing to a different news piece. "I guess she settled."

His spirit sunk. All that work, and a child ended up dying anyway. What cruel injustice.

"Hey man, I found the symbol."

Tom tossed the phone to Logan, who caught it with his right hand. He peered at the screen. The sideways eight was enlarged, with a word beneath it . . .

"Infinity," Tom finished his thought.

"Infinity, of course!" Logan said. "I saw this in math class in college. It's the math symbol for infinity."

"Yeah but what's it mean?"

"I don't know. Four . . . the fourth day of the month, maybe? Or the fourth month?"

"Not the fourth month, April has passed."

"Right."

He tossed the phone back to Tom. He stared at the wall, his thoughts turning rapidly as he leaned against the headboard. He remembered the last time he'd stayed in a hotel like this. Jasmine and he had just got engaged, and he had planned a weekend trip for the two of them. Everything else was perfect. Flowers, a night on the town, stargazing at the park. By the time he got to booking the hotel, he was down to sixty dollars and jumped at first one he could afford. Needless to say, it wasn't the Plaza.

She didn't seem to care, though. Jasmine just smiled sweetly at him, dark waves framing her unblemished face.

"I love it, Logan," she had said. "I love every night spent with you."

His heart had skipped a beat.

She and his unborn child were snuffed out, like wisps of wind that touches the Earth for a moment before disappearing into the air. Now Sophia was dead, and Marianne was worse than dead. She didn't know what she was doing, just as Logan hadn't only weeks ago. Her conscience was being blocked by the evil that dwelled within that contract . . .

A contract he told her to sign. The guilt once again threatened to destroy his insides.

He caught movement in his peripheral. He glanced at Tom, who had grabbed the motel phone, punching in numbers.

"What are you doing?" Logan asked.

He didn't respond. He put the phone up to his ear.

"Hello, I'd like to report a disturbance over at 3427 Gaddy Road," he said. "I heard some screaming coming from there earlier today. I thought you guys might want to check it out."

There was some talking on the other end.

"Alright, thank you."

He hung up the phone.

"Gaddy . . ." Logan said thoughtfully. "That's the road Sophia lives on, isn't it?"

Tom nodded. His shoulders were in a defeated slump. "I couldn't just leave her there. Someone had to know."

Logan nodded to indicate he understood. Tom continued. "I think we should hold our own memorial for her, apart from the funeral. You know, since we're the only ones who know how she died."

"Yeah, I think that's a good idea. We'll have it in the morning."

"Good. But right now, I just want to lay down and forget about it."

"Of course."

Tom sunk into the bed, his eyes glued to the television until they could stay open no longer, falling into a deep sleep.

∼∼

The next morning, a bright, gleaming sun shone across the city, its rays reflecting off of the glass and steel skyscrapers that dotted its skyline. New York City was awake. Traffic formed on the streets, figures traveling along the sidewalks. People talked excitedly to one another, some tourists, others native, all feeling the exhilaration that a sunny day in the city can give.

In the heart of the bustling city, Marianne killed another victim.

She had followed her victim to St. Mary's Church, where the girl had gone early to pray. St. Mary's. One of the churches that Marianne had attended herself. This particular woman, a girl named Kim Morgan, had started a Bible study group and not invited her. So much for loving thy neighbor. The world would be better off without her.

The girl screamed as Marianne stuck a knife into her back, digging it in several times until her shirt was soaked red. Kim collapsed onto the pew in front of her, her hair askew across her face, blood oozing onto the floor. Marianne reached to pick up the body.

"And I thought I was cold."

She whipped towards the sound. Sallos strolled casually down the aisle, his hands in his pockets and his eyes alight with amusement.

"At least my victims know when I'm killing them. But stabbing someone in the back? That's just bad manners."

She was not humored. "You were at the banquet."

He stroked a nonexistent beard. "Yes, I do love crashing parties."

"You're a demon."

"Ah, you are excelling at this game!"

"Don't patronize me. What are you doing here? Keep it brief, I have work to do."

"Yes, I see that." His eyes trickled to Kim's body. "Going to hang it on the ceiling like your other piece of work?"

She smiled. "Something like that."

"Murder. Such an art, isn't it?"

At this, her smile faded. She remembered the banquet, the photo of Emily, the sick feeling that erupted in her stomach. Emily may have been insignificant in the grand scheme of things, but she was the closest thing Marianne had to a friend.

Sallos' presence put a bad taste in her mouth.

"If you're just going to make small talk, then leave. I don't have time for it."

She started to turn away. He glided forward, forcing her to look back.

"I do have a subject that might interest you," he hissed. "It goes by the name of Logan Lokte."

"He is of no concern to you."

"Actually, he is. I was hired by our Master to be concerned. He is an agent of the enemy . . ."

"I'm aware of that."

"He must be eliminated, him and his friend."

Her interest peaked. "You were hired to kill him? Why the trouble? Lucifer doesn't go around killing everyone in New York City. Why him?"

"Because he's directly interfering with her plan."

"You mean my plan." She pondered this, and a sour feeling pitted her stomach. "The Master thinks I will fail."

"Oh don't be ridiculous, Marianne. If she didn't think you could do it, she wouldn't have chosen you. But you are still half-human. And because of that, you are weak."

"I'm not . . ."

"Part of you is weak, whether you like it or not. That's why I'm here. The moment the fool comes near you, I will stick my knife into his heart." He pulled out a jagged knife from his belt, which gleamed in the fluorescent light. "He won't even know what hit him."

There was undeniable glee in his voice. She surveyed him. Blonde shaggy hair, cold blue eyes, strong muscular frame. All was the same as when she had last seen him except one thing: a scar that spread in an open slash along the side of his eye . . .

"This isn't about serving our master," she realized. "You are seeking revenge."

He blinked in surprise. "What?"

A dark excitement lit within her. "Oh, don't deny it. I am the demon of vengeance. I can smell it on you. You want revenge on Logan for something. What did he do, Sallos? Defeat you? Humiliate you? Or is he the reason for that scar?"

She could tell he was restraining himself. "What he did is not important. Just know that I need to kill him."

"Well that's too bad." She took a step back. "Because you can't. I have special plans for that boy. I won't have you ruining them."

"Plans? Are those to occur anytime soon?"

"Perhaps," she smirked.

"I will stick around until then. I'm not particular on how he dies. If you want to kill him, be my guest. But if you can't, just know, I will finish it."

She hated the thought of Sallos hovering over her. "There is no need. I will do it."

"It's just a precaution. Lucifer isn't about to take any chances."

"Fine, but you won't be necessary. Trust me when I say that I will kill him. His blood will run like water in the streets."

Despite her determination, a twinge of doubt flickered within her.

Chapter 23

Logan and Tom stood by the river that separated New York and New Jersey. The water shone in the morning sun, its ripples sparkling like diamonds. Ducks swam, people walked past. As the world rushed by, they felt frozen. Sophia reminded them of their failures, and of the potential horrors that awaited them. Logan inhaled, tasting the light salty breeze. They each held a single white rose. Tom barely noticed the drops of blood where the thorns punctured his skin.

"Sophia was an amazing woman," Logan began, his voice melding into the waves. "She believed in me when no one else could, and took me in at the risk of her own life. That is a debt I cannot repay."

It was Tom's turn. He tried to steady his wobbly legs. "Years ago, when we met, her kindness was the first thing I noticed. Since then she's helped me so much. When my best friend disappeared, she was the one who comforted me. She told me that everything would be alright. Now she's dead because of me. All I can say is that I'm sorry,

Sophia . . . I'm really, really sorry. If we meet again, I hope that you can forgive me."

They leaned down at the same time, bending over the pier and placing the roses gently in the water. They floated away, traveling beneath the overlooking sun.

Away, just like everyone Logan loved.

~~~

Both were quiet as they went through the motel door, greeted by a musty smell and dark tan walls. They collapsed on the beds. Logan grabbed the remote and punched his thumb on the power button. Anything to fill in the silence. The television sprung to life, and a newscaster appeared before them.

This one was a man with bright green eyes and brown hair that was slicked to the side. His bushy eyebrows were pulled together in concern.

". . . The body was found in her apartment, hung up on the ceiling with barbed wire. He was later identified as Christopher Ballard, her talent agent of two years."

They leaned forward. The screen switched to a live scene, where a woman with chocolate skin gripped onto a microphone, standing in front a line of flashing police cars.

"Another victim was found just now in St. Mary's Catholic Church. Though the details are not yet disclosed, the body was said to have been hanging from the cross inside the church. Again, the authorities have not disclosed much, but this could be the work of Marianne Garcia, suspected murderer at large. If you have any information regarding her whereabouts, please call the police immediately."

"Wow," Tom said. "Another one? Marianne's been busy."

"Yeah . . . yeah she has."

Logan stood up and began to pace around the room. He snatched the bible from the nightstand and gripped it tightly, skimming through the pages.

"Dude, what are you doing?"

His thoughts churned. "That's three in three days."

"Yeah, so?"

"So remember how I said that she must have settled with the child? I didn't understand why, but now I think I do. Four. Four, all through the bible except Revelations. Don't you see? It's four people, four days. Four, because the number in the Bible is supposed to represent man. For Mari, it's the fall of man. That's her plan. It's a schedule!"

Tom swung his feet over the bed. "So she only has one left. And it's happening tomorrow."

"Yes."

"Okay, so what's with the infinity sign in Revelations?"

Logan thought about this for a minute. "That's also a schedule."

"Okay, now you lost me."

"Marianne is inhabited by the demon of both vengeance and destruction. Both are for different purposes. Vengeance is what she's interested in now . . . four people, four days to enact revenge on the people who made her feel lesser. After that is destruction."

Understanding lined Tom's face. "The apocalypse."

"Yes!"

"Infinity means . . ."

"Infinite death."

Tom sighed and leaned back on his hands. "That means we have a whole day to stop her."

He frowned. "Yes."

"Man, even I know that's a lost cause. We don't know where she is, or who she plans to kill . . ."

Logan dropped the bible on the bed and started towards the door.

"Wait! Where are you going?"

"I'm going to her apartment to look for more clues. I might have missed something."

"You can't do that!" Tom exclaimed. "She's on the news, the police have probably torn her place apart."

"Well I've got to look. I can't just sit here and wait for her to kill again."

". . . I'll go with you."

"No, you stay here. If something does happen, one of us needs to be able to stop her."

Tom peered at him gravely. "What makes you think we can?"

Logan paused. Unable to come up with a response, he shot him a nod before whipping out the door.

~~~

The familiar door was covered in bright yellow caution tape, and he was once again brought back to Marianne's yellow dress, that smile that radiated like the sun . . .

He wiggled the handle. Locked, of course. He dug into his pocket and pulled out a bended paper clip, which he carried for situations such as this. He stuck the clip into the lock. He jiggled it for a few moments, angling it to the side so that the lock sprung open. He smiled. He swung the door open and dashed under the caution tape.

The police's presence lingered in the room. The curtain around her bed had been torn open, the blood-stained sheets gone. The ceiling was clear, the only evidence being one red stain that seemed embedded in the plaster. He wondered if this place would ever be rented out again. The blood on ceiling seemed like it might be a permanent feature.

He rushed to the couch and ducked his head under, his eyes searching. A voice rung out behind him:

"It's not there."

He whipped to the side. Standing in front of the kitchen was Lucifer, her long red hair forming perfect curls along her neck, her eyes like two hot coals. Her skin was unblemished, almost porcelain, and she wore a long, slinky black dress that fit comfortably around her wide hips. There was something Logan had never noticed before. A smell, like burnt meat rotting in an open field. She glided towards him.

"The phone was taken by the good cops of New York, just like everything else in here. A pity. If only dear Marianne would have checked her phone a few weeks ago. Maybe she would have never signed."

"What are you talking about?"

"About her good agent, Christopher Ballard. He called to tell her she landed the role on Broadway right after the banquet. Oh if only the sweet girl would have known, perhaps she would have chose a different path, and saved herself from such an evil fate!" She snickered. "Oh well."

He ignored her mockery. "How did you know I was looking for the phone?"

He should have known better than to ask, because her laughter rung like a bell. "I am the devil, dear boy! Even in this physical form, I exist in the mind of every living person on Earth. I know every dirty little thought you've had, including those about our good friend Marianne."

"Where is she?"

"Oh, wouldn't you like to know?"

"I do want to know who was calling last time I was at this apartment. It was her mother, wasn't it?"

Cruel amusement lit up in her eyes. "Yes. Mommy is paying a visit to New York. Too bad you didn't answer while you had the chance, huh? You could have spared her from a potentially nasty encounter with her daughter."

"Is her mom the next target then?"

"I haven't kept track of her plans. I have my trusty demons to do that for me." She smiled slyly. "And even if I knew, I wouldn't tell you."

"You know my thoughts, but you don't know hers?"

"I don't desire to know. She is mine, now. She poses no threat."

He stepped forward. "Unless she breaks the contract."

"Like you did?" she asked, her voice quiet and smooth. "That is no longer possible."

"And why is that?"

She strolled over to the window, her hand clasped on the wooden edge. "You created murderers, Logan Lokte. You were never one yourself. She has killed people. A child, even. Even if she could forgive herself, that thirst is a part of her now. There is no turning back."

"I don't believe that. All things are possible with God."

"Well, look at the big crusader. Tell me, what has this God given you? A run-down hotel, paid by a broke friend? The desertion of your beloved? The death of the old woman who you cared so much about?"

"You did those things," he snapped.

"And your almighty God could have stopped it."

"... Even so, He has given me forgiveness."

"Forgiveness? You didn't need forgiveness with me! I gave you everything; a livelihood, a purpose. Grand hotels, all the money you desired. All you had to do was make contracts. Your life was great, Logan."

She walked towards him, her heels clacking against the hardwood. She was close, only a foot away.

"It can be that way again. You say God is forgiving? I forgive the worst crimes, even betrayal. Think of it. No more judgment, no more guilt. You will be free."

Her voice was soothing, tempting, like fresh rain on a hot summer day. But he could still smell it. The burning scent that radiated from her body, like charred flesh . . .

". . . But you never forgave God for kicking you out of Heaven, did you?"

Her eyes widened. She slapped him, and the force knocked him backward. He clutched his burning face.

"You fool! You could have had everything. Now you're going to die like the rest of them."

"You're wrong, I already have everything. Now leave. I am done talking to you."

Her fists clenched together, her skin flushing a bright red. "You dare tell me . . ?!"

"Yes, I dare. Go."

"You can't . . ."

"In the name of Jesus Christ, I command you to leave!"

He blinked, and by the time his eyes opened, she was gone.

Chapter 24

Logan did not return to the motel.

He wandered the streets past groups of people, friendly chatter that was soon to be snuffed out. He didn't know what to do. He had exhausted every resource he could. He didn't know where Marianne was, let alone how to stop her. Perhaps he wasn't meant to. The apocalypse was going to happen at some point. Maybe he should just let it.

He walked and walked, crossing different streets, different neighborhoods. Every dark-haired woman made him do a double take, but his hope faded with each unfamiliar face. He just wanted some idea of what to do. It was like he was standing at the edge of a cliff, and no matter how hard he tried, he could not keep himself from falling. He still loved Marianne. Even if he could not stop the end of the world, knowing that she was free would be enough for him to die with satisfaction.

He walked.

His stops were few. Dirty streets and gutters thick with sludge turned into the grand architecture of Manhattan. Manhattan turned into large, flashing televisions shouting advertisements from the skyscrapers in Time Square. The early afternoon sun began to fall, turning the sky into an explosion of orange, pink and red. When the moon finally rose, a bright orb in an otherwise dark expanse, he trekked to Central Park, where he had sat with Marianne in a sea of green. The only light from lines of dim streetlamps. He sat in that familiar spot, looking out on the water and watching the moonlight reflect on the ripples. Anxiety. Fear. Hopelessness. The emotions coursed through him as midnight struck, signaling a new day. The last day.

He fell face first into the ground. If only he could save her. That was his only prayer, over and over, dirt sticking to his face and the fresh scent of grass filling his nostrils. *Help me save her.*

He lifted his head, and his mouth dropped. A white dove stood in front of him. Its feathers glowed in the light as it stared at him, its black eyes ablaze and seeming to convey urgency. He remembered the dove that led him to the daycare before, and wondered if this was the same one.

His voice shaking, he spoke to the creature: "Take me to her."

It let out a chirp and flapped its wings upward. Logan moved his legs forward as it shot into the sky. He bounded across the grass, onto concrete, his eyes fixed on the little white bird. It led him out of the park and onto the streets, where he had to leap in front of honking cars. Through an alley, along a sidewalk. He ignored the curious looks that followed him.

Soon the streets were recognizable, the buildings familiar. The dove perched on the top of a steeple, the church towering above him in a long, angled point. It was the church where he had regained his soul.

Apprehension dribbled in him, his stomach like a tangled knot. He caught his breath before latching onto the bronze handles and yanking the doors open.

The wooden pews stood before him, moonlight shining through an array of stained glass. A figure stood at the end of the carpeted aisle. A chill went through him. The figure was slim, with long, curly black hair, cascading over a black corset top . . .

Marianne turned around. She smiled when she saw him, a thin sword with a red hilt clutched in her right hand. She stroked the metal. Her voice was as hard as ice.

"Just the man I wanted to see. You certainly saved me the trouble of finding you."

She looked frightening, her black attire seeming to blend with the shadows. He had to think about her words for a moment, before the realization dawned on him.

"Me. I'm the fourth."

"Very perceptive." She tossed the sword to him, which clanked on the ground near his feet. "Betrayal, in every possible way. You are my Judas."

He looked at the sword, then back at her. "What is this . . ?"

"I'm not going to kill you while you're unsuspecting, like I did my other victims. That's too easy. You and I are going to fight."

She pulled out another sword of the same length from her back, letting it dangle at her side.

"I'm not going to fight you," he said.

She smirked, as if she knew that's what he was going to say. "You will if you want to save yourself."

"Oh, don't give him false hope," a man's voice echoed. Logan turned his head towards the back of the church, where a man stood perched in the shadows. He stepped forward, and the white light revealed Sallos. His hair was fashioned messily around his face, a nearly fresh scar illuminated on his left eye. He seemed animated, as Logan had seen him get when he killed people.

"You have an insurance policy."

"Not that I ever needed one," Marianne remarked. Her face was contorted in disgust, and Logan realized that she liked Sallos about as much as he did.

"Sallos." Logan took a step forward. "You look different then when I last saw you."

"And whose fault is that?" he seethed. "In case you have forgotten, it was after babysitting you that I got thrown into the Pit. Nobody comes out of there unscathed."

"If all you got was a scratch, it couldn't have been *that* bad."

Sallos gritted his teeth and began to move towards him. Marianne held her sword in front of him. "Back up, scar face. This is my night."

"You don't have to do this, Mari." Logan held his hands up warily. "Please. It doesn't have to be this way."

"Yes it does, my Judas. It really does. Now pick up the sword."

"Mari . . ."

"Pick it up!"

He knelt down, and felt the cool hilt beneath his fingertips. It was light, like an extension of his own arm. She advanced.

"Please, don't . . ."

The response was immediate. She brought the sword down on him, the metal like a flash of light. Instinct took over as he brought his own sword up, metal clanking against metal.

"See?" she said. "Was that so hard?"

She swung her sword to the side, bringing it down toward his hip. He felt the blade brush against him. She was so strong; it was nothing like Logan had faced in fencing during college. She brought her weapon to his shoulder and he blocked it again, peering into those dark, mad eyes.

"Mari, listen to me! I never meant to betray you."

She swung around, bringing her sword against his. She stepped forward, him back. Back and forth their blades struck, each clang an eruption of sound. He was nearly backed up into the doors, his arms working tirelessly to hold their stance.

"It was you. You changed me!"

She reared her arm back, bringing the sword directly towards his face. He ducked, and it sunk into the door. She tore it free, her jaw set together angrily. Splinters flew from the wood.

"It was your goodness . . ."

She swung at his head. He stepped back, missing the blade by an inch. Beads of perspiration stuck to his body as he brought his weapon up again, then down, and again on each side. She was wild, her strength increasing with each swing. He only got weaker. Eventually they were at the side of the church, wedged between pews and the wall. They voyaged down the narrow aisle, and Marianne brought her sword up against his. The screeching metal held together for a moment before sliding off, the edge of her blade striking the pew next to her.

"I'm sorry I didn't realize it before you asked to sign," he said, chest heaving. "I'm sorry I didn't become the man you deserved."

"A pretty speech from a traitor," she sneered. She swiped at his legs. He jumped, and their blades struck together again. "But as always, you forget Emily."

"Emily?"

Another swing. He dodged it and plunged his sword at her side. A strong block.

"Yes, Emily!" Her penciled eyebrows were pulled into a crease. "You knew she was dead, but you let me go on in ignorance! And even knowing this, you proceeded to seduce me, a love-sick girl who didn't know any better. A betrayal of the most monstrous kind."

"Wait, hold on." He put a hand in the air. "That's what this is about? You're still mad at me about Emily?"

"Of course I am! She was my only friend, and you let her die!"

For a moment, they were both still, the only sound coming from the cool air creeping from the vents.

". . . Mari, I was possessed by a demon. How many Emilys have you killed since your change?"

Her eyes widened.

Sallos watched from the corner, his gaze set on the scene. From there he saw a flicker of humanity flash across Marianne's face, her grip slackening on the sword. He knew it. Don't send a human to do a demon's job, he always said. Such weakness.

Unbeknownst to Logan and Marianne, Sallos slid out his dagger, aiming for Logan's neck . . .

But just before he could rear back his deadly arm, something ran by his peripheral. He paused as a large figure lunged at him, knocking him on the floor and sending his dagger skidding across the hardwood.

Marianne and Logan looked over. Tom stood over Sallos, his lips pursed together defiantly.

"You're not killing anyone else."

"You really shouldn't have done that," Sallos growled.

Tom's knees buckled under him, but he held his ground. Both their eyes traveled to the curvy dagger that glimmered a few feet away. Sallos crawled. Tom leapt. They raced, and Tom began to lose his footing over Sallos' slumped body . . .

Across the church, Marianne had reverted back to anger. She threw her weapon at Logan harder than before, and it took all of his strength just to block her attacks. Again, trapped in this dance of death. Blocking, blocking, blocking. His arms were starting to shake, his legs buckling beneath him. Her hair flew, her teeth gnashed together. How much longer could he last against this enraged demon?

Not just a demon, a cool voice whispered within him. It wasn't like the demon's voice that had plagued him for four years. It was loving. Gentle.

He took a deep breath.

Tom stumbled over Sallos' arm, falling hard onto the floor. He reached across the dusty wood, snatching the dagger just before Sallos' fingers could grip the handle. The demon snarled. He reared the dagger back, but as he tried to plunge it into his chest, Sallos lunged, grabbing tightly onto Tom's arms and pinning him to the ground. Tom's head hit the floor. Sallos began to push down his hand, bringing the knife closer and closer to Tom's exposed neck. The blade traced his jugular, and a small puncture sent a trickle of blood down to his shoulder. The moonlight shined on Sallos' face, shadows tracing his sharp blue eyes, his teeth bared like a predator ready to devour its prey.

"Any last words?" he seethed.

Tom choked against the dagger. ". . . Y-yes . . ."

In a feat of strength, unexpected even to Tom, he started pushing against Sallos' grip. The dagger went up slowly, shaking under the resistance. Sallos' breathing quickened as the blade got further and further from Tom, closer to Sallos' face. The tip looked like it could even be touching his unscathed cheek. But as Sallos focused on his own dagger coming towards him, Tom freed his other hand, bringing it up and clocking Sallos' left temple. The demon fell backward.

Tom took the opportunity to dive on top of him. Sallos was reprimanded, his arms sprawled to his sides in a moment of pure shock. As those cold eyes focused on his, Tom brought down his arm, plunging the dagger into the demon's chest.

Blood seeped from the wound, only the hilt of the blade visible from his skin. Sallos' mouth was open in surprise.

"That's for Sophia," Tom said quietly.

Logan and Marianne stood close together, their swords in a deadly embrace.

"That's what the demons make us do." Logan said. "They make us kill people like Emily."

She swung her blade at his face. He swiped it away.

"You told me before that no one was innocent. Does that apply to Emily, too?"

She let out a cry and jabbed at his side. He leapt out of the way.

"You're not making sense, Marianne. Are there innocents, or aren't there? Did she not deserve to die, just like those other people you killed?"

"SHUT UP!"

Another swing, this one slamming into the wall and breaking the plaster. They were getting closer to the back of the church.

"Why?" he breathed. "It's because you don't know, isn't it? Because you and the demon are at odds about it."

"No!"

She had backed him up onto the steps, to the right of the golden cross. Another swing, another block.

"Grief is a human emotion, Mari! Demons don't feel grief, because grief comes from love, and love is from God."

"Shut up! God never loved me! He abandoned me. He left me with no friends, no success, no hope. Then he tried to take my mother away from me! That's not a loving God!"

". . . You're wrong. God does love you. Just like I do."

He put his arm down, releasing the sword and letting it clank on the floor. She seemed conflicted, her nostrils flared and her eyebrows burrowed in confusion.

"Pick it up," she commanded.

"No. I love you, and I'm not going to fight you anymore. If you want to kill me . . . kill me."

"I said, pick it up!"

"No."

She paused before slowly bringing up her sword. She aimed it at Logan's neck, and he took a deep breath, waiting for it to slice through him . . .

But it never happened. Her eyes widened as she dropped the sword. Her beautiful face was contorted in pain.

"Help me, Logan," she whispered. "I want out."

She put a trembling hand to her forehead, where he was sure a demon was screaming profusely. "Please, help me get out!"

"Okay . . ." He walked up to her and put both hands steadily on her shoulders. "Remember what I said before? A contract can be broken, but only by God. You have to believe again, Mari."

She cried out in pain, both hands pressed against her ears.

"Mari!"

Her eyes were squinted, her mouth open in a silent scream. She looked up at the cross, tears streaming down her cheeks as the gold glimmered in front of her.

"God . . . forgive me."

A crack of thunder. A strong wind blew through the church, the two front doors rattling dangerously against the walls. Logan felt himself being torn from Marianne. His back flew onto the hardwood. Marianne stood in the midst of a giant tornado. The wind swirled all nearby objects, and she screamed as the unseen demon was torn from her body. Her hair flapped around her, her nails clutched at her open face. The wind nearly forced his eyes shut, and he struggled to see Marianne's frame from beneath the gray swirl.

It ended almost as soon as it began. Objects dropped midair. As the wind ceased, Logan rubbed his eyes and opened them wide. He looked hopefully at the woman he loved, who stood with her back to him. But just as he was about to cry for joy, she collapsed onto the ground.

"Mari!"

He rushed over to her. She looked broken, her body sprawled awkwardly on the altar steps. Her own sword protruded from her stomach.

"No, no, no, Marianne . . ." He dropped to his knees beside her. She was shaking, her caramel skin turning a pale white. Blood seeped from the wound. He placed his own trembling hands beneath her head, placing it on his lap.

Shock.

"Tom," he cried. "Tom, call 911! Get an ambulance!"

Tom stood frigidly at the other side of the church. He seemed at a loss, his hands fumbling together.

"Tom, do SOMETHING!"

"I-I can't," he started. "It would just bring the police here. They'll arrest her."

A small cry escaped Logan's throat. He looked back at her. She blinked, her chapped lips parted slightly.

"L-Logan . . ."

"I'm here." Tears streamed from his eyes. "I'm here, Marianne."

The smell of blood filled his nostrils, his tears tasting like salt in his mouth.

"It's gone. Logan, I . . ." She stopped, and her face tightened in a silent sob. "All those people."

"Shh . . ."

"Oh my . . . a child . . . what have I? Oh . . ."

"Shh." He put a gentle finger to her lips. Her body was convulsing, weeping in his arms, though no tears came. "That didn't happen, alright? None of that matters now. I'm here."

His own words came out broken, his cheeks red and his eyes flooding. His chest was tightened with pain, his own breath like forced gasps.

She looked at him. The pain was apparent in her eyes. "I'm sorry . . . I'm . . ."

Her words turned into a violent cough. He stroked her hair softly.

"All is forgiven, Mari."

"Thank you, Logan . . ." Her gaze fluttered upward. ". . . Thank you."

Her eyes shut. She was sheet white when the shaking stopped, and her breathing ceased. All the tension dissipated, her body falling limply in his arms. Cold. She was so cold. No flush to those golden cheeks, no exhale from her full lips. Just stiff and cold.

He cried as he held Marianne's dead body, his scream sounding out through the stained glass church.

Chapter 25

A jumble of words throughout the graveyard, from a minister that didn't even know the deceased. Empty, generic words.

It was an afternoon funeral. The sky was covered with an expanse of gray clouds, where a timid sun peeked from behind. Logan could smell the precipitation lingering in the air. All around, gravestones, and an empty ocean of withered grass. Tom stood by his side. On his right were three people he'd never met, a plump, middle-aged woman, a teenage boy with short trimmed hair, and Marianne's mother, who wept silently at her daughter's grave.

What a job for the minister. Performing a murderer's funeral could not have been the easiest of tasks. Logan could see the precipitation on his neck, the way he shifted on both feet. Would it not be better for her family to speak?

Kansas' rolling hills were visible from the cemetery. So different; so peaceful. Why did people move to the chaos of the city, when they could have the quiet of the country? That's what Logan wanted. Quiet.

As the funeral came to an end, flowers were placed on her grave. Logan and Tom had their own. White roses, like they had for Sophia. They waited their turn in line then placed the flowers in the dirt. Dirt, where Marianne would lie forever.

After he had placed down the flower, Logan moved to where Marianne's mother stood. She wore a cap over her bald head. She had narrow brown eyes and honey skin, her eyes and mouth lined with age. She was an average size, with a small protruding stomach and wide hips hidden beneath slacks and a button-up shirt.

Most importantly, she was healthy. Even with all the horrible things Lucifer did, she did hold her end of the deal.

Her red, puffy eyes turned to him. He was too weary to smile.

"Hi, I wanted to introduce myself. I'm Logan Lokte."

Her lips parted with understanding. "Logan. Yes . . . she talked about you."

"She talked about you too. You seemed really close."

"We were . . ." She choked on her tears. "I just don't understand it . . ."

"Understand what?"

"This! All of this!" She fiddled anxiously with a handkerchief. "When my cancer disappeared, it was a miracle. The doctors couldn't comprehend it. I couldn't either. But as soon I was cured, I called. I called, and called, and called, and no answer from her. Then, all of a sudden, she's accused of murder? I go to New York to find her, and she was . . ." She wiped her nose and peered at Logan imploringly. "You were there with her, weren't you?"

He paused. "Sometimes."

"Then you must know! Please, please tell me. It can't all be true, can it? My daughter, my baby girl. She wasn't a murderer?"

At first, he wasn't sure how to respond. How could he possibly convey the truth? But as he looked into the grieving woman's eyes, the words came to him, like a waterfall.

"Ms. Garcia, I didn't know Marianne long. But the girl I knew was kind. She was gentle, she was loving. Now I can't say what all she did. What I do know is that she was good. That girl, whose cheeks formed dimples when she laughed; who could quote Shakespeare, and who went to the park everyday just to appreciate its beauty. That's the Marianne we remember, and will treasure. She was good, Ms. Garcia. Despite what everybody says, know that she was good, and that she died at peace. Don't ask me how I know. Just know that I'm telling the truth . . . and that she loved you."

The tears leaked off of her cheeks. She squeezed his arm with a trembling hand. "Thank you, Logan. Thank you."

~~~

They were still at the cemetery hours later. Tom sat close to Logan, their legs buried in the hot grass. Logan stared at the headstone: *Marianne Garcia, beloved daughter.* So impersonal.

"You know it's better this way," Tom said quietly. "If she had lived, she would probably be on death row right now."

"I know."

A breeze came through, rippling the hair around Logan's neck.

"I just thought things would be different."

". . . I know."

"I thought things could be fixed, somehow. I thought we could still be together."

He remembered Jasmine and his unborn daughter. The emptiness. The grief. Not understanding how such a horrible thing could happen to innocent people. He had wondered how he could rebuild his life from there. How could he go out again? How could he be happy, even for a moment, with them gone?

The emptiness was still there, like a gaping hole in his chest. But he knew better now. He would be happy again. He had to be.

Though that day seemed light years away.

"What are you going to do now?" Tom asked.

"What I have to. I'll find my parents, let them know I'm alive. I'll grieve. I'll feel like the world is about to fall all around me. But someday, I will move on. And when I do, I have work to do."

Tom tilted his head to the side. "Work?"

"I've got to fix what I have done, Tom. I corrupted a lot of people, tricked them into deals when they were most vulnerable. Now they're slaves to the devil. I can't let that go on. I've got to try and save the people I have hurt."

Tom shook his head sadly, ringlets bouncing around his face. "You know I can't follow you there, buddy."

"I know."

Just as he said this, Tom put a firm hand on his shoulder, an encouraging smile on his face. "But you know I will always be here if you need me."

Despite his grief, he smiled back. "Thank you."

A bit of sun shone through the thick rain clouds. Just a few yards away, a dove flew, soaring upward into the warm, open sky.

Bonus Story Included!

"Unlocked"
A short prequel to *Lokte*

New York City, 1985

"The holy water, Sophia! BRING IT TO ME!"

Sophia Parks obeyed, rushing to the edge of the room where a table stood, various holy relics spread across it. The walls shook. Harsh wind circled the room, lapping her brown, gray-streaked hair around her face. The boy, barely sixteen, was strapped to the bed and shrieking so loud that her ears rung. His face was distorted, eyes dark red, shaggy black hair pressed to his sweat-covered face. The demon that resided within him was stronger than any one Sophia had ever faced. The exorcism had already been going on for hours; adrenaline seemed to be the only thing keeping her conscious. She glanced at Father Peter. His wrinkles were more defined on his gaunt face. The thin white hair on the top of his head dripped with sweat, thick eyebrows pressed together. Still, he kept on, reciting from the bible held in his withered hands, even though he knew the verses by heart.

"We drive you from us, whoever you may be, unclean spirits . . ."

The demon shrieked again. Sophia rushed the holy water to Father Peter, which he flicked on the demon. It screeched as if being burned.

"The Most High God commands you . . ."

"Hypocrite, hypocrite, hypocrite, hypocrite . . ."

The demon repeated the word with violent twists of his head. Father Peter kept on.

"Christ, God's Word made flesh, commands you . . ."

The chill from the wind gave Sophia goose bumps. She said her own silent prayer that the demon would leave before either of them passed out. The demon contorted, the boy's flesh pressing against the red sheets. He cried out again, his voice changing to a menacing dual tone.

"No one commands me, Father!"

A metal cross from one of the tables began to shake. Sophia spotted it from the corner of her eye and leapt towards it. It was too fast. The metal gleamed as the cross zoomed through the air, evading her grasp by inches. The sharp end plunged into Father Peter's chest.

"NOOO!" Sophia screamed.

The demon began to laugh in that cold dual tone. Father Peter placed a shaky hand on his wound, where his own cross protruded from beneath his skin. It came back soaked red. He met Sophia's eyes for a moment, then collapsed.

"Father!"

She rushed to the priest's side, cupping his hand firmly in hers. He was pale, lips trembling slightly.

"I'll call the doctor," she said, and started to get up. He stopped her with a gentle hand. She remained, peering into his bright green eyes.

"You must finish it," he said, voice small under the demon's laughter.

He placed the bible and holy water in her hands. She tried to fight the tears brimming in her eyes. "But Father . . ."

"Please, Sophia."

As much as she hated it, she knew he was right. She nodded briskly. He smiled for a moment, eyes trickling up to the white, speckled ceiling. But the smile soon faded, and his brown eyes glazed over. He was gone.

"Some man of God now, huh?" The demon snickered.

Sophia's insides boiled with anger. She was still for a moment, taking a deep breath as the demon jeered behind her. The ability to stay calm and commanding was key. She had assisted in dozens of exorcisms before. She knew the steps by heart. She stood up, clutching tightly onto the bible and holy water.

"A *woman* trying to perform an exorcism?" the demon howled with laughter. It's teeth had begun to turn black. "Nothing but a filthy, lowly woman . . ."

"Thus, cursed dragon, and you, diabolical legions, we adjure you by the living God." She tossed the holy water at it. The demon screamed as she continued, her voice crisp and clear. "By the true God, by the holy God . . ."

"You can't banish me, woman!" It growled. "You are nothing!"

"By the God who so loved the world, He gave up his only son, that every soul . . ."

"WHORE! FILTHY, LITTLE WHORE!"

"Might not perish, but have life everlasting . . ."

"Sophia Parks, can't be a priest because of that clam between her legs. Sophia Parks, can't please her own husband, in life or in the bed. Sophia Parks, couldn't save her only son."

She paled at the last part. Her head flooded with memories; her eighteen year old son, Joey, enlisted to serve in the last years of the Vietnam War. The soldiers coming to her house, telling her he wasn't coming back. That day had been her worst nightmare coming true.

But that was eleven years ago. Now she had to focus on saving this boy.

"Stop deceiving human creatures," she stated even louder. "And pouring out to them the poison of eternal damnation . . ."

It screamed and contorted. Objects flew across the room, which Sophia was forced to dodge. She continued to say the words, sweat pouring down her face, voice getting stronger every second. The demon continued to spout insults, but she was no longer listening. She gripped onto the bible, glaring at the monster before her.

"Be gone, Satan! Inventor and master of all deceit, enemy of man's salvation!"

"No," it growled.

"Be gone!"

It flung its head back and let out an ear-piercing cry.

"IN THE NAME OF JESUS CHRIST, BE GONE!"

The boy collapsed on the bed. The wind ceased, objects falling straight to the floor. The boy groaned. His face was pale, but no longer blanched, with no black lining his teeth or deep shadows under his eyes. The demon was gone.

~~~

"You can't keep doing this, Soph."

Sophia turned toward her husband. His blonde hair was streaked with white, deep lines embedded beneath his blue eyes. He pursed his lips at her, straightening the red tie that hung over his suit. She thought back to the twenty-nine years they'd been married. It had been great up until the death of their son. That's when Sophia finally decided to pursue a bigger role in the church, assisting Father Peter at every waking opportunity. Her husband Gerard was very vocal about his feelings toward it. Too vocal, she thought.

"Gerard, can we not do this today?" She straightened her skirt, gazing in the mirror at her all black attire. She hated funerals, especially when they were for someone she cared about.

He took a step forward. "Father Peter was killed by a demon you faced. This easily could have been your funeral! When are you going to get it? Exorcisms are too dangerous."

"Would you be saying this if I weren't a woman, I wonder?"

He flinched at the low jibe. "Of course I would. And I hope you would tell me the same."

"I wouldn't do exorcisms if I didn't have to. I'm not about to turn away people who ask for help, Gerard."

"It's not your responsibility to help everyone."

"Actually, it is."

"Yeah, well I don't think that's the reason you do it."

"What are you talking about?"

His gazed turned downcast. "Look, sweetheart, I know things have been rough since Joey died . . ." She stiffened at the sound of her son's name. "And I think you were looking for . . . I don't know. Some kind of thrill? Something to focus on? Which is great. I love that you have an outlet, but it's just too dangerous for me to stay silent about it. I . . . I can't lose you too."

She was about to say something sarcastic, but the sadness in his tone warned her not to. ". . . I wish there was something I could say to make you feel better, but I know that to do that, I'd have to say I won't continue doing my service for the Church. And I can't. I'm sorry."

His eyes narrowed to slits. "Then for God's sake, let me do it with you."

"No," she said, turning away.

"Why not?"

"Because I know what I'm doing. You would just get yourself killed."

"Father Peter knew what he was doing, and that didn't save him!"

He seemed to regret it immediately after he said it. She felt her face grow hot. Oh, how she wanted to curse at him, to tell him he didn't have a clue what he was talking about. Instead she looked down at the floor.

"Let's just go."

~~~

Sophia forced herself not to cry at the funeral. She had cared for Father Peter. She had only begun assisting him in exorcisms due to their deep friendship and his trust in her. She longed to go back; change it, somehow. If only there was a way to bring back all the people she'd lost . . .

She willed the thought away, lest she begin crying.

As she sat stiffly in the uncomfortable church pew, she felt a pair of eyes on her. She slowly shifted her gaze. In her peripheral she could make out a woman standing in the back of the church . . . staring at her. Sophia could no longer focus on the words being said at the service as those eyes bored into her, never leaving.

When the service ended, Sophia bolted toward the back, leaving her dumbfounded husband behind. The woman was still there. She was quite pretty, with a natural type of beauty that Sophia herself had never been blessed with. She looked to be in her mid-twenties, with long dark hair and big brown eyes red from tears. Her pale skin was luminous in the light, pink lips pulled together. In her dainty hands she wrung what looked to be a cloth headband. Sophia walked up to the woman, who continued to stare. The woman opened her mouth as if to speak, then closed it.

". . . I caught you watching me during the service," Sophia finally said. "Was there something you needed from me?"

"Y-yes . . ." the woman stammered. "Sophia Parks, right? You assisted Father Peter."

"Yes, and who might you be?"

"Oh, sorry, I'm Demi." She offered an awkward smile, then turned her gaze on the floor. She bit her lip, as if she wanted to say something but was too afraid to.

" . . . Okay, Demi, how about you just tell me what you need? I promise I'll believe you, and I won't get upset or dismiss you as crazy or whatever sour reaction you think I'll have."

Demi looked up, eyes wide. "Oh. Well, it's just, I heard you have experience with, you know, demons." Sophia nodded, and Demi continued. "It's just that, I think I have one, and . . . It followed me here."

Sophia blinked in surprise. She was about to reply when her husband came from behind, white-gold hair hung slightly over his face. She felt annoyance creep within her.

"I must have lost you in the crowd there," he told his wife with a beaming smile. His gaze shifted to Demi. "I don't believe we've met before. I'm Gerard, Sophia's husband. And you are?"

"Nobody," she said quickly. "I'm nobody, I've got to go . . ."

She began to leave. Sophia called after her, and shot Gerard an icy glare. He gave back a look of confusion. Sophia raced after her, weaving through crowds and bursting out the large chapel doors. She saw Demi on the sidewalk trying to hail a taxi. She moved forward, bones aching from the excitement. She grabbed Demi's frail little arm and she whipped around, tears streaming down her face.

"Stop, I can help you!" Sophia exclaimed, panting. "Just tell me more."

Demi shook her head quickly. "No, you can't."

"Why not?" People began to leave the building. Gerard had stayed back, which Sophia was thankful for.

"Because," Demi continued. "I thought, since you perform exorcisms, that you must not have a family. I thought . . . But I can't let you help me and risk hurting your loved ones. You could die."

"Well of course I could die, that's how dealing with demons is," she replied, dumbfounded. "But I do it because I don't want anyone else to die. I'm certainly not going to let *you* die. Okay?"

Demi seemed like she was about to argue, but then nodded quickly, her face sticky and red with tears. She looked at Sophia for a moment and hugged her. Sophia was startled at first, but slowly put her arm around her, giving her a small pat on the back.

"It'll be alright," she soothed. "I'm going to let my husband know what's going on. You stay here, okay? I'll be right back."

The woman sniffled and nodded. Sophia turned around, pushing past the exiting church crowd, eyes scanning the chapel. Gerard was off to the side. She walked up to him.

"Gerard, you're going to hate me for this, but that girl needs my help."

His blue eyes narrowed. "Demon-type help?"

She nodded. He sighed and put a weary hand behind his neck. "I know you won't listen to me about not going, so I'm not gonna try to convince you on that. But please Soph, please let me go with you."

She started to say no, then stopped, peering deep into her husband's eyes. Aged. Wise. Loving. As much as he and she argued, she couldn't deny how much she deeply loved him. For eleven years he'd been asking her to stop doing exorcisms. Perhaps it was time to show him what they were all about.

"Fine," she said with a sigh. "But just be prepared, because I'm not sure what we're dealing with yet."

~~~

Demi glanced behind nervously as they entered the cab. "It was there, I saw it," she said, rubbing her hands together. Sophia and Gerard exchanged looks. She knew what he was thinking. He was wondering whether the girl was crazy.

Honestly, so was she.

They arrived at a modest dark blue house. A white front door greeted them, its edges chipped away. It almost looked as if the house was squished, for it was tall and vertical, pressed between two other tall houses. The inside felt just as vertical as the outside. A set of carpeted stairs stood right in front of the doorway. A narrow hallway led to a tapered kitchen, a dining room, a comfortable-looking living room, a hallway closet and a half-bath tucked beneath the stairs. They settled in the living room as Demi brought them hot coffee. Sophia put the cup to her nose and inhaled, the scent of fresh coffee filling her nostrils. She took an eager sip.

"Do you live alone in this house?" Sophia inquired politely.

"Yes. Well, no . . . sort of. My boyfriend stays over a lot, but he's on a business trip right now."

"Hmm. And why do you think a demon is following you?" Sophia asked, setting her cup on the table. Demi shifted uncomfortably.

"Well, I've been having these dreams of demons trying to kill me, or drag me to hell. At first, I thought that was all they were; dreams. But then . . ."

"Then what?"

". . . Then I saw one from my dream. In real life."

Gerard glanced at Sophia. He definitely thought she was crazy.

"Did the demon approach you?" Sophia asked calmly.

"No, he was watching me. He looked like . . . I don't know, like he wanted to kill me. I figured I was just imagining things, but then last night, some weird stuff started happening. The lights started flickering, the doors were banging, the television went to static. I tried to call the electric company, but all I could hear on the phone line was this sharp ringing sound. I even unplugged the television. The static was still there. I was so scared . . . I tried to run out, but the doors were locked. So finally I just locked myself in my bedroom and closed my eyes until it all stopped. And it did. All at once. I've never seen anything like it."

Sophia leaned forward with interest. Gerard had a hand over his mouth.

"I thought I was going insane. But then, right after it all stopped, I saw him. He was right outside my window, staring at me with those cold brown eyes. Just when I was about to scream, he smiled at me. It was the most chilling smile I've ever seen. He said, 'see you, tomorrow, Demi,' and then he was gone." She looked down. "I didn't sleep last night, and I spent all this morning and afternoon at the library researching. That's when I found you. I was going to get Father Peter, but then I learned his funeral was today . . ."

Sophia sprung to her feet, pacing. Demi looked up at her. Fresh tears fell down her cheeks.

"He's coming again tonight, then," Gerard said, eyes flickering to the setting sun behind the curtains.

"Yes," Sophia replied. Her mind was racing. "What I don't know is what the demon wants, and that is crucial. Demi, have you experienced anything odd before this incident? Strange cravings, weird smells? The feeling someone is watching you, but there's no one there? Voices?"

She seemed to think about this for a moment, then shook her head.

"It's not possession then . . ."

"What could he want?" Demi asked, face red. Sophia's heart pounded. She had only ever dealt with possession; the other stuff she had simply read about.

"I'm not sure," she began. "Perhaps he wants to invoke you into a deal with the devil. Maybe you were given to him as an assignment. Or maybe, he is just wreaking havoc."

Gerard frowned. "Are any of those a more likely option?"

"I don't know, it's hard to say. I've never worked with a case like this before."

"I thought you did exorcisms," Demi said.

"Yes, exorcisms, which are for demon possession. I'm unsure how to handle non-possession cases."

Demi groaned, causing Sophia's confidence to falter. Gerard's eyes were soft. He looked as if he wanted to comfort her. Instead he stayed silent. She clenched her teeth together, a dull, throbbing pain spreading through her temple.

"I'm afraid I can't be of much help until I know more. I have a few methods I could try. If I could just see the demon . . ."

At that moment, all the lights to the house turned off, causing Demi to gasp. A bright moon peeked behind the curtains, providing only enough light for them to see one another's shapes. Nobody moved. For a long, tense moment, heavy breathing was the only sound. But then, a shadow passed by the window. Sophia saw a flash in Demi's direction; she must have been covering her mouth. Sophia squinted at the curtain. A tall, muscular silhouette stood behind it. Sophia did not have to see him to know he was the demon. She could feel the evil radiating from the doorway. His posture seemed casual, and Sophia wondered if he was smiling.

"Deeeemmmii," the smooth voice cooed.

Demi gasped, and Sophia shushed her. The absolute glee in his voice was enough for Sophia to know that he planned on hurting Demi. She put her hands in front of her and felt for Demi's thick sweater.

"Hide," she whispered. "Now!"

Demi did as obeyed, disappearing up the stairs.

The demon taunted them with a knock on the door.

"Soph, we have to get out of here," Gerard whispered, panicked.

"No, it will just follow us. You hide. I'm going to get rid of it."

"No."

"Gerard, really . . ."

"No, I'm not going without you."

She heard the creaking of metal as the doorknob turned slowly. Her head spun. She needed to see exactly what they were dealing with, but there was no way she could do that with Gerard in harm's way. She sighed and grabbed the hulking arm she spied through the dark. He followed silently as she raced him out of the living room and into a hall closet. Just as they disappeared inside, the front door swung open.

Heavy footsteps echoed against the floor. Sophia tried to push down the anxiety that was building within her. She had to stay calm and have faith in God. That was key.

She heard the front door latch behind him.

"Oh, Demi, I didn't know we were playing hide and seek," he said, sounding amused. "You have me quite ill-prepared, but I suppose I'll play. Oh, and do Sophia and Gerard want to play too?"

A trickle went down her spine. She gripped onto the cross sticking out of her purse.

"Such chaos," he mused. "To kill the innocent . . . or at least, those who appear to be. For no one is truly innocent, are they, Sophia?"

Her breath caught in her throat, and she felt Gerard's firm hand clutching her shoulder. He was toying with them the same way every demon she encountered did. Still, something he said bit at her, as if she had missed something very important . . .

"Who shall I find first, I wonder? My target, the sweet and gullible Demi, her weak incapable protector, or the protector's cowardly husband?" The steps were so close, Sophia felt herself stiffen. He was right beside them. ". . . Let's see what's behind door number one!"

She nearly gasped. The door directly across from them had been yanked open, and she knew he must be looking at an empty bathroom. Shoes shuffled across the floor. He had pivoted in their direction. She gripped so tightly on the cross, she thought she may bleed.

"Perhaps door number two, then?" his breath echoed against the wood. She instinctively tried to shield her husband, her heart beating so fast it seemed to bang against her chest. She heard the doorknob squeak, and within a moment, the door opened.

She whipped out the cross, holding it to the demon's chest. He backed up, hands held out.

"And she comes out swinging!"

She gazed at his face in the darkness. He had a strong jaw and dark, cruel eyes. His hair was shaggy, his skin a darker shade. Middle Eastern descent, perhaps?

Most demons feared the cross, but this one gazed straight into Sophia's eyes, a smirk etched at the corner of his mouth. She tried to ignore her unease.

"I command you, demon, in the name of Jesus Christ, leave this place!" she cried.

He closed his eyes for a moment. He then opened them and smiled.

"That's cute."

He knocked away the cross so fast she didn't have time to react. His hand was around her throat in a flash, and she felt herself being lifted off the ground, her feet dangling above it. She took strenuous breaths through her nearly closed windpipe. Fear encompassed her.

"There are some demons you just shouldn't try to face," he seethed.

He threw her, and she felt her body sailing in the air briefly before her side bashed into the wall. She crumpled to the carpet, breath coming out in gasps. Everything hurt. But what hurt most of all was her left arm. She tried to move it and screamed in pain. It was at least fractured, maybe even broken. She looked up to see the demon taking a step towards her.

"GET AWAY FROM HER!"

"No, Gerard . . ." she tried to yell, but her voice came out strangled. Gerard moved towards the demon in a long, brisk stride. He threw a punch at the side of his head, but the demon blocked it easily, grabbing his fist and squeezing it tight. Gerard winced under his grip. The demon smiled, pulling out something long and shiny from his pocket. It was jagged around the edges, coming to a fine point at the end. A knife.

She tried to yell again, but no sound came out. In a flash, the demon shoved the knife into Gerard's stomach. Gerard gasped as the blade pierced his side. The demon withdrew the knife, and blood began to seep from his shirt. Sophia stared in disbelief as her husband fell to the ground, a trembling hand placed over his wound.

The demon looked between the two of them. "Well that was just too easy. Remind me next time to not be so hasty. Takes the fun out of it." His cold eyes traveled upstairs. "Two down. One to go."

"No . . ." Sophia watched as he ascended up the stairs. She crawled, pulling herself with her good arm towards her husband's body. He was still alive, but barely, his breathing ragged. Seeing

Gerard like that made Sophia's heart feel like it might explode. Hot tears streamed down her cheeks.

"I'm so sorry," she sniffled. "This is all my fault . . ."

He put a gentle finger to her lips. "No. I'm sorry . . . I-I should have . . . protected you . . ."

He coughed, and blood spilled on his lip. She held onto him tightly.

"Sophia . . . You are everything to me. I love you so much . . ."

"Hey, now." She tried to smile, but it felt forced. "You're making it sound like goodbye."

He looked at her. His eyes seemed to twinkle in the darkness. "We'll see each other again, my love. I promise . . ."

He looked at the ceiling and the tension in his body ceased, the light dissolving from his eyes. Tears rushed down Sophia's face, her cheeks wet and sticky. It felt as if she may break in half. It seemed impossible, yet it was right before her eyes. Her husband was dead beneath her. So many years they'd been married; so many times she had taken him for granted. And now she would never get to tell him how much she cared, how much she always had . . .

Rage bubbled inside her. She looked toward the stairs. She could hear the demon's steps echoing throughout the hall, that infernal voice ever jeering. She pushed herself onto her feet. She wobbled for a moment then steadied herself. Her left arm hung uselessly at her side. She didn't have a plan; just the desire to banish that murderer once and for all.

"Father God, please help me expel this demon."

She walked quietly up the steps, feet sinking into the carpet. She could hear the demon clearly, raging about destruction and chaos. But where was Demi hiding?

She reached the top of the steps and peeked from behind the wall. There was nothing but darkness, all the doors in the hall ajar. He must have been checking the rooms one by one. Sophia crept along the hallway, shadows cast upon her face. He was still talking- it seemed he never stopped- and she followed the smooth voice to the room at the end of the hall, slowly looking into it. Demi's bedroom was barely visible in the night, the pale moon shining through sheer curtains. Her queen sized bed was perfectly made, the comforter lined with cheery flower designs, the only other décor being two nightstands on either side. There seemed only two places she could hide; the closet at the side of the room, or under the bed. The demon paced around the room like a wolf. His eyes were menacing in the moonlight.

"Nowhere left to run, Demi," he hissed.

Did she still have a pocket knife? Sophia dug into the purse that still hung loosely over her shoulder. Bible, wallet, pens, paper . . . Aha! She closed the cool metal within her fingers. She longed to leap at him right then. Instead, she waited within the shadows. She had to catch him off guard.

He walked slowly to the edge of the bed, kneeling down like a tiger. He clasped onto the bed skirt, and Sophia felt her breath catch in her throat. He yanked it up. He sneered and let the skirt fall back down. Demi was not under there. His eyes flickered to the closet.

"I know where you are, now."

Sophia's mind raced. If she attacked him now, Demi may have been able to run. But his side was facing her. He'd be expecting. She had to wait until his back was turned . . .

He approached the closet doors slowly, each step seeming meticulously planned. He grasped the white knobs, and Sophia balanced on the balls of her feet. He threw the doors open.

Demi was there, cowering against the wall. She held a bent, extended hanger in front of her. He smiled. "Hello."

Sophia leapt into the room. He had just looked in her direction when she sent the knife into his shoulder, withdrawing it instantly and causing blood to ooze out. He cried out and clutched the wound. Demi inched out of the closet, hanger in front of her, hair sticking to her tear stained face. Sophia got her bible out as the demon whipped to face her. His gaze was like knives.

"You . . ."

"Most glorious Prince of the Heavenly Armies, Saint Michael the Archangel, defend us in our battle against principalities and powers, against the rulers of this world of darkness, against the spirits of wickedness in the high places..."

He closed his eyes for a moment and clenched his jaw. Hope began to rise in Sophia. She continued, becoming more forceful with each word. But instead of continuing to show pain, his eyes opened. He looked straight at her. He raised his fist and brought it down on her face.

White flooded her vision. The pain knocked her to the ground, head banging against the carpet. She grasped the floor with her good hand and coughed. She spat out blood and, to her horror, one of her teeth. She put her fingers to her throbbing cheek. Her jaw wasn't broken, which she supposed was a miracle itself. He kicked her stomach, and her abdomen exploded with pain.

She barely looked up. Demi had begun to run, but the demon grabbed her around the stomach, hoisting her up. She screamed and thrashed. He held a strong arm around her, locking her arms in place. He sniffed her hair, and she trembled.

"How about we have some fun first, huh?" he sneered.

Demi whimpered. Sophia tried to get up, but was greeted by another flood of pain. *It's not supposed to end like this,* she thought desperately. *Please, Lord, please don't let her die...*

The demon flung her onto the bed. Her side crashed into the lamp on her nightstand, knocking it over with a crash. He was on top of her in a flash, stroking her face with his knife. He smiled devilishly.

"Shall we begin?"

Suddenly, there was a woman standing behind the demon. What? Sophia blinked, thinking she must have suffered some severe head trauma. But then the woman grabbed the demon's arm. He looked up, and his eyes widened with fear. The woman flung him across the room like a doll. The closet doors splintered beneath him.

Sophia gazed at the woman. She was tall, with long red hair that formed into beautiful waves down her back. She wore a black dress that hugged her curvy hips, red spiky heels planted in the floor. She had a tight jaw, skin pale and luminescent as the moon. Her eyes, streaked with eyeliner, were like fire. She was a demon, and a powerful one. Sophia could feel the authority radiating off her slender body.

"My liege," the demon whimpered. His shoulder was streaked with blood. "I . . ."

"Do not bore me with an explanation, Sallos," the woman snapped. "You have disappointed me."

"But, my lord . . ."

Sophia's head spun. Sallos. That was the demon's name, then. He seemed invincible before, but now he cowered beneath this woman like a dog. Sophia could not wrap her brain around what this meant.

The woman lifted Sallos to his feet with one hand, setting him roughly on the ground. Though he greatly exceeded her in size, his head was bowed low, and he dared not meet her eyes.

"You know you must consult me before killing," she said, gazing at him as if he were an insect.

"I know, I . . ."

"You are a loose cannon, Sallos."

She placed a polished hand on the wound on his shoulder. She dug her thumb into the cut, causing Sallos to grunt in pain. Sophia winced. The woman's thumb disappeared halfway into the wound. How deep had Sophia cut him? Just as Sallos had begun squirming in pain, she retracted her thumb and slapped him hard with her other hand. He stumbled. Her nails left sharp cuts in his skin. He started to reach toward his bloody gashes then stopped, placing his arms respectfully at his sides.

"You are not to touch her unless I give the word. I have plans for her." She looked at Demi, eyes tracing along her abdomen. Demi shivered.

"Yes, my lord. Forgive me."

"Unlikely." She grabbed Sallos' arm, causing him to wince. She looked back between Demi and Sophia, her eyes sharp.

"See you soon."
Their bodies flickered, and within seconds, they were gone.

~~~

"Sophia!"

Sophia looked down from her front porch and smiled. Demi had just pulled on the curb and was walking up to Sophia's steps. She was radiant. Her skin seemed to glow in the sunlight, her eyes shining like stars. It was late fall, and a chill seeped through the holes in Sophia's over-sized sweater. Still, she preferred the outside. It had been three weeks since Gerard's passing, and she still wasn't used to the house being so empty. At least outside there was life.

Demi walked onto the porch and took a seat on the chair across from her. Demi had been making frequent visits to Sophia, a couple with her boyfriend tagging along. At first, the visits irritated Sophia. She didn't want to be pitied. But then something happened, something she didn't expect: she and Demi became friends.

"How are you doing today?" Demi asked, teeth flashing.

"Not too bad today, Demi," she said with a small smile.

"Good! Any changes? Have you decided what you're doing with Gerard's stuff?"

Sophia thought of all her husband's possessions sitting around the house. She had always teased him about being a hoarder because he collected so many things. He would defend himself with, 'You never know. We may need this someday.' Now there was so much stuff lying around she hadn't been sure what to do with it.

"I think I'm going to keep it," she replied slowly. "Put it in the basement, at least. Who knows? Perhaps I'll use some of it someday."

Demi nodded and bit her lip. She was leaning forward in her chair, leg bouncing up and down. Sophia raised her eyebrows. "Do you have something you want to tell me?"

A smile broke out on Demi's face. A slight blush rushed to her cheeks. "Yes. I mean, no. It's just, it's good news, and I don't want to trouble you with it. Things have been so hard for you . . ."

Sophia dismissed her with a quick wave. "Nonsense, you can tell me anything. Now, what is this good news?"

Demi looked down then back up, eyes sparkling. "I'm pregnant."

She felt a stab of pain mixed with excitement. She thought back to when she was pregnant with Joey, how happy she and Gerard had been . . .

No. No painful memories, not while Demi was there.

Sophia smiled at her. "That's wonderful news."

She beamed. "We are so excited! Oh, and he asked me to marry him. Can you believe it? A baby and marriage all at the once. I could dance with happiness!" She looked down at her belly, where a faint bubble protruded. "That woman . . . that demon said that she had plans for me. You don't think she would try to hurt my baby, do you?"

There was genuine concern in her eyes. Sophia shook her head. "No, darling, and even if she did, I would protect you both. Count on it."

Demi gave a small smile, but Sophia could tell she was still worried.

"So have you thought of any names for the baby?" Sophia asked, changing the subject.

"I don't know. I really like the name Logan for a boy. Logan Lokte . . . has a nice ring to it, doesn't it?"

She thought about it for a moment. "Yes, I think it does. Logan Lokte."

About the Author

K.J. Bryen lives in Oklahoma City with her loving husband, Adam, and two crazy dogs. She loves any book that immerses her into a world she doesn't want to leave, and she hopes to be able to do that for her readers. She's also a coffee addict and a Joss Whedon fanatic. Every one of her books is dedicated to a different charity. *Lokte* is dedicated to the A21 Campaign, to help victims of human trafficking. Feel free to check out her other upcoming works at her website, www.plungingintothenovel.com.

Made in the USA
Charleston, SC
10 November 2014